D1269741

Look for other *Show Strides* books:

#1 School Horses and Show Ponies

#3 Moving Up and Moving On

2

Confidence Comeback

series created & Written
by
Rennie Dyball

Illustrated by
Madeleine Murray

The Plaid Horse
Canton, New York

Copyright © 2019 by Piper Klemm
The Plaid Horse, Canton, New York

Library of Congress Control Number: 2019902660
Show Strides: Confidence Comeback / Piper Klemm
Text by Rennie Dyball
Illustrated by Madeleine Swann Murray

This is a work of fiction. Names, characters, businesses, places,
events, locales, and incidents are either the products of the author's
imagination or used in a fictitious manner. Any resemblance to actual
persons, living or dead, or actual events is purely coincidental.

ISBN 978-1-7329632-1-4

Illustrations © 2019 by Madeleine Swann Murray
Cover Art by Lynn Del Vecchio

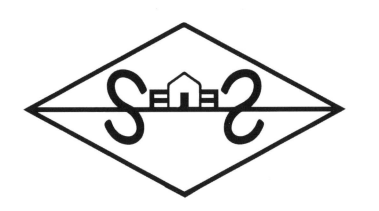

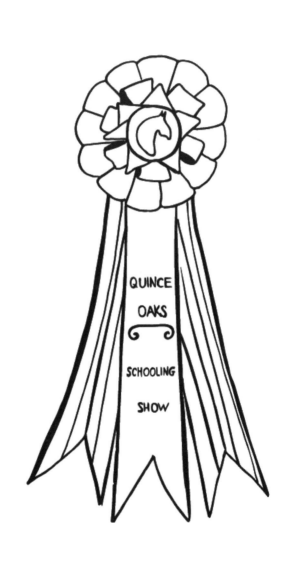

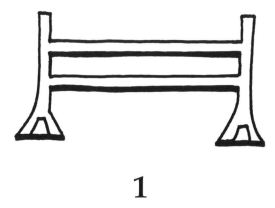

1

"Make your comebacks stronger than your setbacks."

As Tally put her pony's tack away, she frowned at the "Quote of the Week" on the chalkboard inside the Field Ridge tack room. They'd just gotten back to the barn after their disaster of a first show together.

At the very first jump—at Tally's very first A-rated show—the pony she was catch-riding, Stonelea Dance Party, refused the fence and Tally fell off. When Danny (as he was called at the barn) ducked hard to the left, she went right and flew over the jump alone. Seriously upset and embarrassed, she somehow managed to keep from crying in front of her new trainer, Ryan, as well as everyone else watching. Ryan brushed the footing off Tally's jacket and led the pony out of the ring. Then he gave Tally a pep talk about how everyone falls off at a show sometimes. Even the very best riders.

After Tally fell, Isabelle—a sixteen-year-old client of Ryan's who'd shown earlier in the day—did a warm-up round on Danny to school him, getting him over all eight jumps. Ryan nodded approvingly and gave Danny a big pat as they left the ring. Then he made Tally get back on to jump a few fences in the schooling area.

"He dogged you at that first jump, so I wanted Isabelle to get him around and remind him about the job he needs to do," Ryan told Tally. "Now I want you to get back on in the schooling area for your confidence."

Tally and Danny popped over a few jumps together, including a jump that Ryan purposefully set up to look spooky by adding a cooler to the top rail with his puffy vest draped on top of that. Tally felt the pony stare it down and hesitate a few strides out. "Sit, and leg!" Ryan called, and Tally rode definitively to the base of the fence. Danny peeked down a little bit, but Tally felt calmly in control and confident that they'd clear it. After that mini-lesson in the schooling ring, it was as if the show ring blunder had never happened. She thought back on it bitterly as she flicked on the tack room light so she could wipe down Danny's bridle in the fading afternoon light. She looped the throat latch through the end of the reins and fastened it, then wrapped the noseband around the whole bridle, pulling the buckle to the front and feeding the tapered end of the leather through the keepers. A month ago, she'd never heard of this figure-eight technique for storing bridles.

She'd learned a lot in a short period of time since she started riding with Ryan and catch-riding Danny, but it all ended in embarrassment that late fall morning. Tally kicked the tack trunk by the door in frustration, like a little kid. She'd definitely suffered the "setback," as someone phrased it on the white board. The problem was, with no home shows at her barn on the schedule—and an uncertain future with catch-riding in general—she had no idea when she'd have a chance for the comeback.

2

"Hey! You left the show too quickly. I was looking for you."

Tally's new friend, Mac, who boarded a pony named Joey at Oaks, joined her in the tack room.

Miserable as she felt, Tally still hoped the show had gone better for Mac (short for Mackenzie, a fun coincidence since Tally's name was short for Natalia).

"How did you and Joey do?"

"Good, we got around and I only chipped at one

jump this time, not like my usual three or four in a course," Mac said, beaming. She was an eighth grader at a private school not far from Tally's middle school, and the girls had become close friends while riding and hanging out at the barn together. "We got a bunch of thirds. Yellow's our color."

Tally noticed the ribbons peeking out from Mac's backpack and suddenly felt terrible about her performance all over again. Before she could try to stop herself, the tears began spilling down her cheeks, and she covered her face, turning away from Mac.

"Oh no, Tally, I'm sorry!"

"Don't be," Tally quickly replied, rubbing her eyes as if she could physically stop the tears at the source. "I'm so happy for you guys. It's just really embarrassing, what happened to me."

"I've fallen off at shows before, it's the worst," Mac said, hugging her. "Actually, I fell off at the first jump once, too, when we got my children's pony. He didn't even stop, it was just a bad chip and I had no balance. I was so short that my feet barely went past the saddle so I'd just go flying off, like, every other ride."

Tally couldn't help but giggle at the image of Mac, a rider she so admired, going flying off a pony. It was awkward—and pretty funny—to cry and laugh at the same time, and Tally suddenly felt quite grateful to have a friend who could turn her tears into laughter.

The next day, Tally had a lesson on her favorite school horse, Sweetie, and she got to the ring early to walk a couple laps to prepare herself for whatever Ryan might have to say about the show. Tally began riding at Oaks five years ago with one of the beginner instructors. Then she moved on to Meg, a more advanced instructor who taught her to jump and coached her at the Quince Oaks schooling shows, which were held in the barn's large indoor arena. But when Meg took a job at her college in Florida, Tally had to start fresh with Ryan. He was a big-time trainer with clients who rode on the A Circuit, so for Tally it was new and exciting to ride with someone so accomplished, but also a little scary. Ryan demanded nothing less than the best out of his riders. You literally had to strive for perfection in every single lesson. Each ride was a chance to do things correctly.

"Hey, Tal," Ryan said as he walked into the indoor. He waved at one of the boarders who was flatting her horse at the far end as he signaled

Tally to walk Sweetie over toward him.

"So. Let's talk about the horse show."

Well, he's not wasting any time, Tally thought to herself.

"Stuff happens. Right? The pony dogged you and that's why I had Isabelle get on him. Ponies do this stuff from time to time. I don't think he's cut out for the children's at this point in his career—he just doesn't have it in him to be forgiving enough. But Isabelle has a ton of experience with ponies who act naughty, and for his training it was important that he get around every jump."

This was a bit of a relief for Tally to hear, as she had anxiously imagined that Ryan might have just given up on her completely. Even at the time, it was helpful to watch a more experienced rider school Danny to work through the problem.

"You rode well on the approach to that jump, but a few strides out, you really leaned up," Ryan continued. "And Danny took advantage of that. So we're going to work today on letting the jumps come to you and not anticipating. Danny may still have stopped at that jump at the show if you hadn't leaned, but I think you might have been able to recover and get back in the tack to try it again."

Tally trotted both directions and then asked Sweetie to canter. The mare took a bunch of rushed trot strides before transitioning into the canter.

"Stop, stop! Start that all over. Not a good transition at all."

Tally gathered up her reins and went to signal Sweetie with her outside leg when Ryan stopped her again.

"Do you feel yourself tipping forward? That's

not going to get a clean transition out of her. Your outside leg should signal her outside hind to step into the canter. Now try it again and glue your butt to that saddle until she's cantering."

Tally and her friends liked to joke that nothing ever got by Ryan. It was the reason they loved riding with him, and why they occasionally dreaded it, too. You simply couldn't get away with doing things in a sloppy or lazy way. But considering how happy and confident his horses and riders looked at home — and the slew of tricolor ribbons on display in the tack room from shows — it seemed like his method was working.

Engaging the mare at the walk, Tally sat a little deeper in the saddle before signaling with her outside leg, making sure to hold her body upright until she got the mare cantering. She had to fight to keep from tipping ahead. Sweetie stayed round through her back and stepped into a canter underneath Tally.

"Better!" Ryan said. After she cantered to the left, he added, "You know, Tal, you can't think of horse shows as, 'I'm gonna ride really well today because I'm at a show.' Think of your lessons that way. Things can be unpredictable at a show, so focus on nailing it every time you ride with me at home."

The other riders who usually took this lesson with Tally both had to cancel today, so Tally had Ryan's full attention. For better or worse. He had plenty more feedback when she and Sweetie cantered to the right.

"Pull your shoulders back . . . right there . . . but don't let your lower leg slip forward. Relax your lower back as you sit the canter. Elbows in. Lower leg back again."

It was a lot to think about.

"Every rider develops bad habits and we're gonna work

together to undo them," said Ryan.

When they started jumping, Ryan was quick to point out each time Tally got ahead with her upper body. Usually, when he gave her direction in a lesson, she could feel what he was talking about. But she didn't seem to notice herself leaning forward for some reason.

"Do you feel your upper body coming forward and everything tipping toward her neck?" Ryan asked her.

Riding was all about feel, so Tally decided to put aside her embarrassment and be honest with Ryan.

"No," she said softly, looking down at Sweetie's martingale strap.

13

"There's no wrong answer here, you're learning! Tell me what you are feeling when you come out of the corner."

Tally thought a moment before answering: "I guess I'm just thinking about the jump and how I'm going to ride it."

Ryan nodded and lowered the jumps in the outside line from verticals down to little cross-rails.

"I think you're anticipating the jumps so much that you're subconsciously getting ahead of the horse. It probably happens more when you're nervous, like at the show. Remember: you've got to let the jump come to you. I want you to add a stride here and canter this line that's set for five strides in six. So, trot in and then canter out. I don't care if you get left behind, and now that the jumps are so little, you don't need to do a whole lot with your body. No big crest release here, just allow."

Tally went to pick up her canter but felt herself lean forward. So she sat back in the saddle to regroup. Sweetie flicked an ear back in her direction. Tally took a breath, sank down into the tack, and asked again, this time keeping her upper body tall and her seat in the tack. Sweetie responded with another clean transition and Tally held her medium pace through the turn toward the line.

Tally fought the urge to perch in the saddle on their approach and did her best to pretend that the jumps weren't even there. When they got to the base of the cross-rail, Tally followed the mare's mouth and tried not to think about what the rest of her body was doing. She counted Sweetie's strides, sitting deeply to collect her canter to get the add—since the line was set as five strides, but Ryan wanted six.

"Halt straight!" Ryan called after they jumped out of the line. Tally kept her deep seat and held her leg on as she asked the mare to slow to a halt.

"Pretty good. You got the six strides, but did I say to canter in? Quit with that. I'll see you next week."

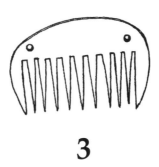

3

Apparently, Tally was no longer capable of holding back tears. She was practically sobbing as she took off Sweetie's bridle, feeling more frustrated with riding than she had in a long time.

"Tough lesson?" Mac asked from Sweetie's doorway. Her friend certainly had a knack for showing up during her emotional moments.

"I can't do anything right," Tally said miserably.

"Hang on . . . I may have a surprise for you," Mac said. "Meet me on the boarders' aisle in like, fifteen minutes?"

"Sure," Tally said, carrying Sweetie's tack out of her stall.

After wiping a sweat mark out of Sweetie's coat, Tally followed the horseshoe shape of the barn around from the riding school aisle to the boarders' aisle. When she got there, Mac was standing with her pony, Joey, who was tacked up on her left. On her right stood a fully tacked bay pony with a snip on its nose.

"This is Beau. I was supposed to hack him for his owner Marion, but I texted her to see if we could take him on a trail ride instead. She said yes. Come on, you need this."

After a quick check-in with her mom about getting picked up later, Tally was aboard. Beau's owner had a seriously comfortable saddle that seemed to hold her lower leg perfectly in place while still allowing her a close feel of Beau's sides as he moved underneath her.

"Joey's a total follower out on the trails, so you go ahead. Marion said Beau's good being in the lead out here."

Tally leaned back to help Beau balance as the ponies ambled down the steep hill that started the trail. At the bottom of the hill, they were just a few yards away from a small stream. Tally kept her legs firm around Beau's sides, just in case he might have a strong opinion about the   water. But he cruised right through it, splashing softly, and Joey followed.

"You want to trot?" Mac asked and Tally's pony immediately transitioned to the new gait. It caught Tally off guard for a moment, and both girls laughed as she quickly regained her balance and began

19

posting.

"Ponies always remind us who's really in charge," Mac joked, and Tally nodded in agreement. It occurred to her that there was no correct diagonal out on the trail so she posted on one diagonal for a while as the trail remained flat and then changed to the other just to keep things even. The woods were so quiet; the only sound was that of the ponies' hooves crunching through the dead leaves. They were well into fall now, so the leaves that remained on the trees ranged in color from yellow, to orange, to bright red.

"Duck!" Tally called back to her friend as she pushed an eye-level branch out of the way, knowing it would snap back at Mac. She glanced over her shoulder just in time to see Mac flatten herself down on Joey's neck to avoid the branch.

Riding freely in the woods was a feeling of such freedom, such joy, that the botched horse show suddenly seemed very far away.

The girls soon arrived at an incline and they slowed their ponies to a walk and then a halt.

"We going up?" Mac asked behind her.

"If we go up this hill, the trail loops around and we can head back to the barn the way we came," Tally said, familiar with the route from group trail rides on the school horses.

"Let's do it!" said Mac.

Tally nudged Beau to walk forward and dropped her weight further down into her heels, knowing that horses and ponies can travel up hills easier the faster they're going. She felt Beau lean back into his hindquarters before springing forward, picking up a canter as they ascended the hill.

Tally grabbed mane and hung on as Beau cleared the steepest part of the hill, slowing to a trot and then a walk as they got to the top. She inhaled deeply and rubbed the pony's neck as they walked on down the trail. Tally felt so happy just to be up in the saddle, enjoying a crisp fall ride outside.

4

The day after Thanksgiving, Quince Oaks was being transformed into a holiday wonderland. Tally worked at the barn so she could earn extra riding lessons, and during her Friday shift she was tasked with hanging sparkly gold and silver garland on each of the school horses' stalls. Oaks, as riders called it, was a unique horseback riding facility. It housed about thirty school horses for its lesson program on one aisle (the right side of the horseshoe-shaped barn) and the aisle on the left was reserved for boarders' horses. There was an entrance to each aisle from the parking lot. The horseshoe shape of the barn curved around an indoor arena, and there was also a larger indoor up the hill from the barn, with an expansive outdoor sand ring immediately adjacent to it.

Tally loved everything about Oaks and was happy to take on some work to earn rides beyond the weekly lesson and occasional schooling shows her parents provided for her. Through Ryan, and by watching her new pal Mac, Tally also got a taste of what it was like to show on the A circuit. Ryan had been giving Tally lessons on his sales pony, Danny, up until just last week. But Danny had been purchased by a rider from a different barn who was moving up to the regular pony hunter division.

Hanging the garland on the stall of a school pony

named Little Bit (or Lil), Tally found herself wishing for the same thing she'd been focused on since that awful show with Danny a few weeks ago: another chance to catch-ride for Ryan.

Lil pinned her ears as Tally secured the silver garland in a U shape across the mare's stall.

"You'll get used to it," Tally told her with a giggle as she continued hanging the garland. When she got to Sweetie's stall at the end of the aisle, she selected one of the remaining gold garlands and secured it to the little chestnut's door. She slipped inside to feed Sweetie some baby carrots she'd stashed in her pocket. Tally had been riding Sweetie for over a year and the pair had a special bond. Grumpy and mare-ish at times, the 14.3 Thoroughbred cross (or 15 hands, depending on who you asked) seemed to want to do her best for Tally, and Tally felt she had a good sense of how to get the best out of the mare as well. With her stature and smaller stride (very small horses were lovingly referred to as "honies," for their similarity to ponies), Sweetie wouldn't be able to get down the lines at the bigger shows. Still, Tally loved competing with her at the Oaks schooling shows.

"Did you roll today?" Tally asked the mare, using a curry motion with her fingers to work through a patch of caked dirt on the horse's neck. Sweetie pinned her ears halfway but seemed to stop herself, as if she thought better of the unfriendly gesture.

"I'll groom you for real later," Tally said, giving the mare a scratch in her favorite spot.

By the end of Tally's shift, Sweetie was clean (or, at least, no longer caked with mud) and the entire school aisle was decked out with the metallic garland. Another working student named Kelsey had outfitted the tack room door and the staircase leading up to the office with Christmas lights and holly, giving the entire aisle a warm, festive glow.

"Wow, you guys outdid yourselves," Brenna, the Oaks barn manager, told them as she emerged from the office. "Thank you so much, it's beautiful. Tally, could you just water the boarder aisle before you go today?"

"Sure."

"No rush, just before you head out."

Tally walked past the tack room out to the open end of the barn where bleachers lined the short end of the indoor ring. Mac was taking a lesson along with another boarder on her horse, and Tally sat down to watch the end of it before finishing up her night filling the water buckets in the stalls of the boarder aisle. As Mac walked past on Joey, Tally gave her a little wave, and Mac rolled her eyes dramatically, nodding toward Ryan.

Mac liked to joke about how hard it was to ride with Ryan, but Tally knew she enjoyed putting in the work—and it paid off. Mac and Joey were steadily improving in "the division," the term riders and trainers used for the regular pony hunters, in which small ponies jump 2'3"; medium ponies, 2'6"; and large ponies, 2'9" or 3'. Mac seemed to average about one show a month and it was fun for Tally to watch her friend progress, even if she did feel the occasional pang of jealousy.

"Better, Isabelle," Ryan said to the other rider. "Okay, Mac, hit it. Get that ring pace first and then sit chilly."

Tally watched as Mac picked up her canter in the corner and legged Joey until he was traveling down the long side of the arena at a good clip. Joey's straight-legged canter movement always reminded Tally of the time she saw the Rockettes in New York City with her parents at Christmas. As Mac guided Joey through a gymnastic down the middle of the ring—they appeared to be working on straightness in this lesson—Tally realized why her friend had rolled her eyes. Mac's saddle, like Isabelle's, was missing its stirrups. Tally was seriously impressed. Dropping her irons in lessons was one thing—removing them from the saddle entirely was quite another.

"Halt straight!" Ryan called out when Mac was a couple strides out of the combination and she responded by sitting even deeper in her saddle, her legs long at the pony's sides, as they slowed to a halt.

"Good, Mac. Tired yet?"

"Yes!" Mac and Isabelle both answered him, and Tally laughed, prompting Ryan to nod in her direction.

"Don't laugh, Tal, you're next."

5

"Walk on over here so I can take off your stirrups. I didn't really make you do much for No-Stirrup November and we're going to make up for that today."

Tally must have tensed all of her muscles because Sweetie responded by lifting her head in the air.

"It's okay, girl, just ignore me," Tally whispered to the mare as she guided her over to Ryan.

"Mac is ready to finish out the month strong. Right, Mac?" Ryan asked, and Mac nodded. Her stirrups had been removed from her saddle for a while now, stored in her tack trunk.

In the middle of the ring, Tally lifted her legs out in front of the saddle while Ryan swiftly removed her stirrup leathers and irons.

"Okay, go pick up your posting trot."

Tally and Mac trotted around for a few laps, bending Sweetie and Joey to the outside on the short sides of the ring and slightly to the inside on the long sides.

"Tally, go ahead and sit. Mac, you keep posting. Both of you, think about relaxing through your hips and thighs while holding your calves still against your horses."

Tally could hardly believe how winded she felt after just a few laps but tried to focus instead on feeling Sweetie bending in response to her cues. School horses were sometimes more resistant to exercises like lateral movements, but Sweetie was generally a willing participant—one of the reasons Tally felt lucky to ride her.

There was still a little gymnastic set up in the middle of the ring from Mac's last lesson, as well as two single verticals on either side. It reminded Tally of the schooling ring at the horse show.

After a quick walk break, both girls and their mounts were ready to start jumping.

"Come right to this little combination, girls, following each other. Trot in, canter out."

Tally couldn't remember the last time she jumped without stirrups, but Ryan seemed to read her mind as she turned toward the combination.

"Just keep that trot you've got and allow through the gymnastic. The jumps are tiny, Tal, you've got this."

And he was right. Sweetie popped over the three cross-rails, one stride between each, and Tally kept her arms soft to follow while focusing on holding her lower legs against Sweetie's sides. Mac rode through the combination next.

"Perfect!" Ryan told both of them. Then they took turns jumping the singles, halting, and trotting into the combination once more.

When it was Tally's turn, she had to canter most of the way around the ring before approaching the first single vertical. Her muscles burned as she worked to not sit too heavily on Sweetie, who told on her by hollowing her back and pinning her ears.

"Ah ha," Ryan said as she made the turn for the single. "You aren't able to get ahead of your horse and anticipate the jumps without your stirrups. I'll remember this!"

As painful as that idea sounded, Ryan was right. Without stirrups, it was much harder to perch ahead of the pommel and anticipate the jump. And so, the jumps did just come to her. Even when she saw her distance a few strides out, there was nothing to do but maintain Sweetie's canter and wait.

"I think this was your strongest lesson so far, Tal," Ryan told her as the girls cooled out their mounts. Tally beamed—Ryan rarely gave out this type of high praise. "Come find me after you put away that horse, okay?"

Mac and Tally walked another couple of laps before dismounting.

"I feel like a cowboy," Tally joked, walking exaggeratedly around Sweetie to loosen her girth.

"I know. I was so scared of No-Stirrup November, but it didn't end up being as bad as I thought.

After the first few lessons, anyway."

"Wait . . . you haven't had your stirrups at all this month?"

Mac looked like she was calculating in her head.

"I don't think Ryan realized it was November for the first week, but he took off our stirrups after that and it's been like, five lessons. So yeah, pretty much the whole month."

Fully in awe of her friend, Tally parted ways with Mac, exiting the indoor ring at the gate by the rounded end of the barn. She and Sweetie turned right toward the school aisle while Mac and Joey went left.

After untacking and brushing Sweetie, Tally returned to the indoor to find Ryan on the phone, seated in the director's chair he'd set up next to the combination. The hunter green material matched that of the coolers on the boarder aisle, and "Field Ridge" was embroidered in script across the back support of the chair. Tally loved all the little personalized touches.

"Okay that sounds good. Talk to you soon," Ryan said before ending his call and addressing another rider in the ring.

"I'll be right with you, go ahead and start trotting around."

Then he turned to Tally.

"I just wanted to let you know that I have some new sales ponies coming to the barn in the next few weeks, including a greener one that I think might be a good fit for you to ride."

Tally could hardly believe what she was hearing. She felt the familiar lump in her throat and burning in her nose that usually signaled she was about to cry.

"Well that's not quite the reaction I expected," Ryan said teasingly.

"It's just . . . after I fell off at the show I didn't think . . . I mean, Isabelle took over the ride so I wasn't sure you'd want me to . . ."

"Look," he said, clapping Tally affectionately on the side of her arm. "To be a good, well-rounded rider, you need mileage. And the only way to get that is to just keep riding. New ponies and horses, different types of ponies and horses, showing at home, doing the bigger shows away from home . . . it all adds up to literal miles in the saddle," Ryan said. "You just didn't have the mileage to push Danny past that bad behavior. Isabelle's got that mileage and experience, so she was a better fit for Danny those last few weeks he was here, in order to get him sold. You did a lot right on him. You've got the feel for riding naturally. I'm proud of you, and I know it's tough to fall at a show, but it's obvious to me that you're making progress."

Her cheeks bright red and her stomach fluttering with excitement, Tally thanked Ryan and walked out of the indoor with the biggest smile.

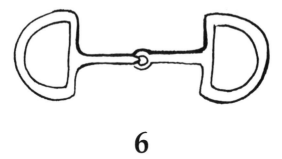

6

The next day at school, Tally sat down for lunch with her friends Kaitlyn and Ava. Kaitlyn also took lessons at Oaks, and Ava used to own Danny before she decided to pursue gymnastics like her older sister. It seemed like a good move for her, too. Ava was always a good rider, but she really seemed to find her groove in her new sport.

"C'mere, I want to show you this before the lunch teachers notice I have my phone out," Ava told the other girls. Their middle school had enacted a strict emergencies-only rule for cell phones after the lunch and study hall periods became dominated by kids on their phones.

Tally and Kaitlyn sat in front of Ava and looked down at her phone in the hopes of blocking the teachers' views. On the screen was Ava from the previous weekend, wearing a sparkly blue leotard and doing what looked to Tally to be impossible flips and turns on a narrow balance beam.

"My coach sent me this today and I was so excited, I had to show you," Ava whispered. "I'm already moving up a level, which she says is rare for someone with my experience."

"Girls! This is your one and only warning," one of the lunch teachers barked at them from across the cafeteria. "Unless, of course, there's an emergency I should be aware of?"

Ava rolled her eyes, and Tally turned red for her.

At the barn that afternoon, Ryan told Tally and some of his other students that he would be going back and forth to Florida during the winter to look at some horses. Come January, he'd also be there with clients to show on the winter circuit, so he encouraged them to ride as much as possible while he was in town.

There was a new lesson schedule in place for the winter, and Sweetie was being used in a jumping lesson right after hers, so Tally was riding Scout. The bay gelding was so friendly and simple compared to her sassy mare, Tally thought with a smile. She tacked Scout in his stall and led him up the aisle and outside to the large indoor. When they passed Sweetie's stall, Tally said hi and the mare stuck her head out over her stall guard expectantly, pinning her ears as Scout passed her.

"Don't be grumpy, girl, I'll come see you after my lesson."

Tally, Mac, and Jordan all rode together that afternoon and worked on jumping three fences set in an S pattern.

"I love this exercise because you can't anticipate and lean up," Ryan told them. "You have to sit up, you have to look, you have to steer. Tally, lead us off. Start with the vertical here, then turn right to this little white gate in the middle of the ring, then turn left and catch the red wall on the far end."

Tally signaled the big bay to pick up his right lead, happy to notice that she didn't have to think about keeping her seat down in the tack now. She wasn't chasing Scout into the canter the way she'd gotten into the habit of doing on Sweetie. She steered him

43

to the first vertical, looking past it to the gate. Three strides out, she trusted her pace and began to set up the second jump by keeping her outside leg to jump on a slight angle. In the air over the vertical, she opened her inside rein slightly and kept her outside leg on so Scout would know where he was going.

"Good, Tal! Did you guys see how she set him up there?" he asked Mac and Jordan.

Tally willed herself not to get distracted by the compliment and focused instead on the second jump, sinking into the saddle and lining up her approach to the gate, with a slight right-to-left bend.

"I don't care how many strides here, just keep the canter the same."

Despite being considerably taller than Sweetie, Scout's stride wasn't much longer, so Tally counted nine strides to the gate and put her new outside leg on and slightly opened her inside rein. Scout felt a little stiffer with this change of direction and landed off the gate straighter than she wanted.

"You want to change the bend sooner there," Ryan said as Tally bumped the gelding with her right leg to move him back over for the red wall. She counted another nine strides to the final jump.

"Not bad," said Ryan. "Mac, hit it."

When it was her turn to jump the exercise again, Tally put her outside leg on Scout sooner and aimed at the second jump on more of an angle. The gelding bulged less in response and they met the third jump without Tally having to overcorrect.

"Better," Ryan said, and Tally patted Scout's neck happily.

After the lesson, once Tally untacked Scout and put his blanket back on, Ryan found her on the school aisle.

45

"Have time to hack the new one?" he asked.

"I do!"

"Great. Follow me around to the boarder tack room and I'll tell you his deal."

Tally walked fast to keep up with Ryan, who talked to her as he headed toward the boarders' aisle. Ryan has a huge stride, Tally thought as she jogged to keep up, laughing at herself for comparing her trainer's gait to that of a horse.

"So, his name is Goose and he's green. He's a small pony but he's big-bodied, and really covers the ground. Interesting story behind him, too—he was born in somebody's backyard. They didn't know that their mare was pregnant and then, boom, they have a colt." Tally nodded eagerly. She wasn't used to riding a horse or pony who had a back story like this one. It felt more like something that would happen in a movie.

"The pony hung out in their backyard until he was four, and then for the last two years he's been working with a trainer who got him backed, trained his lead changes, and got him jumping small courses. She doesn't have the room in her program or a rider for him, though. I'd like to see if we can't make him into a solid show pony. What do you think?"

Tally could barely get the words out in response. "I'd love to! I mean, to flat him. Or show him. Or lessons, or whatever you think . . ."

Ryan's eyes crinkled as he smiled. "Let's take it one step at a time. I'm teaching a lesson up in the big indoor in a half hour. Why don't you hack him up there then so I can keep an eye on you two?"

"Great! Thank you, Ryan!"

"Thank you, Tal, see you soon. He's in the stall next to Joey's. Head on over there and I'll make sure

47

the saddle pads I want are set up with the rest of his tack."

Tally felt her heart thumping wildly in her chest. Ryan went into the tack room, and Tally hurried to the top of the aisle and peered into the pony's dim stall. It took her eyes a moment to adjust, and when they did, she literally gasped at what she saw.

7

"Oh my gosh, Goose, you are gorgeous!" Tally whispered. The pony perked his ears and took a couple of tentative steps toward her. He was a dark dapple gray—gray horses and ponies got lighter in color as they aged; Goose was obviously quite young, with a neatly pulled, silvery mane and the most adorable dished face. He had a pink muzzle and looked cozy in his plaid blanket. Meeting him reminded Tally of opening model horses on Christmas morning and marveling over just how perfect they looked. And here she was, in the stall of a pony just like that. Only this one was real.

Tally gave Goose a scratch on his forehead before going to the tack room to collect the pony's tack and brushes. Ryan had a college-aged working student who was meticulous about labeling everything. Tally felt, yet again, a wave of gratitude for her work, since it saved her from having to ask someone to show her where things were every five minutes.

As Tally brushed the pony, she first took off the front of his blanket to groom that half, then replaced it and pulled up the back half to groom. Goose was body-clipped, and she didn't want him getting too cold. She quickly noticed just how curious he was. Maybe it was his age, or the fact that she was a new person to him, but he took great interest in everything from the soft brush she ran across his neck to her coat when she bent over to pick out his feet. At first, she jumped when he placed his head on the small of her back—a flinch that came from years of grooming certain schoolies who'd try to nip you when you weren't looking. Goose looked mildly offended when Tally flinched, so she rubbed his neck and told him it was okay. When she picked out the other front hoof, Goose tentatively placed his chin on her back again and Tally giggled quietly. She finished getting the pony ready, the two of them quietly enjoying each other's company.

"Hey, Tally," Isabelle said once Goose was tacked and Tally was leading him out of his stall. "Oh, wait a minute, he'll need a quarter sheet."

Tally had no idea what she was talking about, but just a moment later, Isabelle emerged from the tack room carrying a small striped blanket.

"I actually, um, I'm not sure how to put on . . ."

"No worries," Isabelle said breezily, and showed Tally how to thread the pony's tail through the braided loop in the back and pull up the sides of the blanket underneath the flaps of the saddle, securing the whole thing in front of the pommel with Velcro tabs. "Have a good ride!"

Tally walked Goose up to the path toward the large indoor. The pony moved slowly beside her. He was calm, but he took his time checking things out, like a stray lead rope left in the grass, as they made their way up the hill. He also paused to greet one of the full-time grooms who was walking down the hill toward the barn.

Ten minutes later, Tally had walked Goose around the ring on a loose rein, and then once more, picking up some contact with his mouth. Ryan told her to trot the pony around, do some circles, and generally just let him see the ring.

Tally picked up the trot and was immediately taken aback by what the pony felt like underneath her. It was not at all what she expected out of a small pony, a full two hands shorter than the mare she was used to riding.

"What do you think?" Ryan asked. "He's pretty special, huh?"

"There's just . . . so much stride," Tally replied.

Ryan chuckled. "Yeah, he covers a lot of ground. Tons of stride. He measures 12.2 so he's technically a small, but he's really big-bodied, so he probably rides a lot bigger than he actually is. Keep circling and bending him and let him see the ring. Oh, and don't get any taller, okay? You just barely fit on this one."

Tally smiled and kept trotting around on Goose. Though she had hacked Danny at least a dozen times, the concept of flatting a pony herself—without the usual instruction and direction of a lesson—was still a fairly novel one. She felt so special making circles around the jumps and guiding this fancy little newcomer around while Ryan taught another student.

As for the pony, he behaved under saddle a lot like he did on the ground. Giving his surroundings a careful look, but doing so calmly. He had a lot to observe, but without actually spooking. Tally changed directions and sat an extra beat to change her diagonal, grinning to herself at what it felt like to sit just an extra beat of this pony's huge trot. She couldn't imagine having to do a sitting trot on him.

After tracking right and trotting several more

circles, Tally let Goose walk and patted him on the neck.

"When you're ready you can canter both ways, Tal. I'm going to jump her around," Ryan said, nodding at his student. "So just keep an eye on where we're going. You'll be fine on the rail. But I want to make sure Lil' G there is used to the activity of other horses in the ring."

What a cute nickname, Tally thought, steering the pony out to the rail. Picking up the left lead canter, she was surprised at how smooth he felt, and easy to sit. G's canter reminded her of Danny's. It almost felt like riding a rocking horse, with the back-to-front movement. Tally sank down into her heels and sat lightly in the saddle. She thought about keeping the pony from leaning into the bridle and getting heavy on his front end. When Ryan's other student walked in between jumping exercises, Tally put the pony onto a circle, feeling his greenness for the first time. G (the nickname stuck fast) bulged hard to the outside rather than automatically bending around the circle the way she was used to with other rides. On their next circle, Tally put her outside leg on early and opened her inside rein to guide him around.

After cantering a few laps to the right and practicing a couple of transitions from the trot, Tally thought G had put in a good hack and walked him out on a loose rein.

"When you work your next shift, hop on him again," Ryan told her. "Pick a ring where there's other people and do the same thing you did today. Maybe add a serpentine and some simple changes. Nice job today. Keep at it."

8

After another couple of flat rides on Goose by herself, Tally had her first lesson on the pony scheduled for Friday afternoon. She was so excited to jump him. While she recognized the feeling of a big, rocking stride from riding Danny, it was somehow different on Goose. The way he covered the ground just sort of . . . happened. It felt like he was just skipping along, without a care in the world.

"That's what you want in a pony who will do the division one day," Isabelle had told her when they were in the tack room together. "That ground-covering stride feels good to ride, doesn't it?" Tally agreed with her, feeling very lucky to help bring the pony along.

Once Tally finished flatting in her first lesson on Goose, Ryan adjusted a line and told her to trot in and canter out in five strides.

Tally was surprised, and as usual, the emotion showed on her face.

"What's up? That sound okay?"

"Totally," she quickly answered. "I just thought we'd be starting with little cavaletti or something."

"Always a method to my madness," Ryan told her with a wink. "Just keep your leg on to the base, and then when you land, sit chilly, focus on keeping him straight. If you get five strides, six strides, I don't really care. I want straightness and a consistent canter. Let's see what we got."

Tally picked up her trot and concentrated on keeping G between her leg and hand before turning him toward the first jump of the line, a small cross-rail.

"Keep your eye up, Tal, aim for the middle."

Tally did as Ryan instructed and G popped up over the fence, cute as can be. He landed cantering slightly to the left. Tally pulled on the right rein to correct him and he skewed a little too far right. She finally got him straight one stride before the vertical and he gave it a nice, lofty effort.

"Not bad, but you need to steer him with your legs a lot more if he's wiggly down the line. Your hand isn't going to fix that; this needs to come from behind. Do it again."

The next time, Tally jumped in and corrected G's wiggles with her leg signals—she was pleasantly surprised to see that she didn't need to use the reins much, if at all—and he stayed straighter this time trotting in and cantering out in the five.

"Much better! Now do the same thing and then turn left and come up over this little vertical," Ryan said, lowering the single jump on the diagonal. G navigated the five-stride line even better this time, with Tally having to do less to keep him straight. They cantered through the turn, and once G got his eye on the diagonal single he surged forward a little. They met the fence too close and G popped over it in an uncomfortable chip.

"You rode that whole thing great until three or four strides out from the last jump," Ryan said as Tally slowed the pony to a walk. "He changed the pace on you and went past the distance, which is why you chipped. Try it again and if he does the same scoot forward; think about balancing. You don't want to just grab a hold of his mouth because he may take you too literally and think you want him to pull up. Just settle him softly and quietly with your hand while still supporting him with your leg."

G breezed through the outside line again, as if some of his greenness had evaporated over just a few efforts. Tally kept him straight and balanced away from the jump and through the turn. When he picked up the pace again on his way to the single vertical, she squeezed her fingers around the reins and sat tall, keeping both legs lightly on his sides. The pony slowed down just enough that, after a couple more balanced strides, they met the vertical much better.

"Good, Tal, that's the ride! You've got such a nice feel, and I think this guy knows his job pretty well already. Go ahead and quit with that, tell him he's a good boy."

Tally dropped the reins just in front of the pommel and patted G on both sides of his neck, a gesture the pony seemed to appreciate with a long stretch of his neck and a contented, whuffling sigh. Tally quickly gathered the reins back up, a little surprised at herself for trusting an animal she barely knew enough to let go of both reins like that. But it felt like she'd been riding Goose for much longer than she actually had been.

Tally took her time cooling out the pony, grooming him and working out the light sweat marks around his girth area from their lesson. After replacing his blanket and feeding him a handful of baby carrots, she hurried over to the tack room where she changed into a dress, down vest, warm tights, and booties for the Oaks year-end event, which was being held in the little hall on the property. The hall was typically used for indoor activities during Oaks' summer camps, but tonight it would be the setting for the show series awards.

Tally walked around to the school tack room, the meeting spot she'd designated with Kaitlyn, who was also getting a year-end award. Both girls laughed the minute they saw each other. Their outfits were almost identical with their gray puffy vests, gray booties, and black tights.

"Did you girls plan that?" asked Brenna with a wink as she passed them on the aisle. Giggling and planning their next shopping trip, the girls walked out the main entrance and down a little hill to the hall.

Inside, more of the holiday garland and Christmas

lights had been hung up, giving the room a festive, twinkly glow. Before taking their seats, the riders helped themselves to cookies, cheese and crackers, and hot apple cider. Tally almost didn't recognize some of the riders without their helmets.

At the front of the hall, Brenna gave a little speech about everyone's hard work over the six shows of the year. It was fun to have the element of surprise— Tally, like all the other riders in the room, didn't know where she'd end up until the awards were announced and ribbons handed out. But having missed two of the shows in the series, her expectations weren't too high for a top finish.

After Brenna's speech, Tally and Kaitlyn went to get more cider and chatted with Jordan.

"I can't wait for the next show season. Too bad it doesn't start until April," Kaitlyn said.

The memory of Tally's failed attempt at showing Danny still stung when her mind wandered back to it, but it was satisfying to think about the progress she'd made with Sweetie over the course of the Oaks show series.

Seated again, the girls listened as Brenna called out the names of the younger kids from the barn, who happily hurried from their seats to where the barn manager stood at the front of the hall so they could collect their ribbons and prizes. And the rumors were true: the ribbons were extra long and fancy, and, depending on what place you got, accompanied by a small prize.

When it came time for the low hunter division prizes, Tally clapped for the sixth-place winner, then fifth place. It had been a pretty full division in all three shows she rode in, so when Brenna announced the fourth-place winner, one of the boys who rode at Oaks, Tally could hardly believe it. She'd finished in the top three!

"Third place," Brenna said, pausing for dramatic effect, "is Sweet Talker, ridden by Tally Hart." Blushing, as usual, Tally collected her long yellow ribbon, adorned with "Low Hunter Year-End Award" in gold lettering. As Tally thought about where she might hang it in her room, Brenna handed her a leather bracelet embroidered with the words "Quince Oaks Year-End Winner" on it.

Sitting back down with her friends—who'd finished third and sixth in their respective divisions—Tally felt happy, but couldn't shake a negative thought that came with it. Sure, the Oaks shows were fun, but they didn't really compare to the "real" shows she'd gotten to see through Mac and Ryan.

What did it mean to get ribbons at her home shows when there was a whole world of horse shows out there with bigger, better competition?

9

"What are you doing for New Year's?" Mac asked Tally as they walked their ponies around the small indoor ring. It was the first Saturday after Christmas and the temperature had barely climbed above thirty degrees. It was sleeting outside, too, so the girls were taking extra time to walk their ponies. None of the animals got turned out when it was this cold and wet, so it was important to warm up the ponies properly after all that time standing in their stalls.

"Probably watching the ball drop on the couch

with my parents. Really exciting," Tally said dryly.

Mac laughed. "Me too. Wanna sit on the couch together and maybe watch horse show videos instead?"

"Yes! That sounds so much better."

The sleet on the roof of the barn made a pitter-patter sound, and Tally wondered whether it might make Goose nervous, but he didn't seem to notice. His attention was on Tally as she worked on circles and serpentines, keeping him focused as they flatted around. She'd had another couple of lessons on Goose and he was just so eager to try whatever was asked of him—even Ryan seemed impressed with this little green pony. They were jumping small courses in their lessons and G was doing great. He still wiggled down the lines, but it was becoming muscle memory for Tally to steer him with her legs and he got straighter each time. The method to Ryan's madness, as he'd put it, seemed to be moving the pony right along.

After flatting Joey and G, the girls agreed to text that night after confirming the plan with their parents.

Tally's dad picked her up from the barn that afternoon and she asked him right away if Mac could come over to watch horse show videos.

"Is that like watching game tape?" her father asked.

"What's game tape?"

"Well, like football players, for example, they watch game tape—videos—from their games to look back on what they did right and what they can improve. You probably learn from watching these competitions, right?"

Tally nodded.

"I think it's great that you're spending so much time riding and studying the sport," her dad continued.

"It's really admirable, the way you're giving it your all. I'll double check with Mom, but it's fine with me if Mac comes over and stays the night for New Year's. You guys do your thing."

The next night was New Year's Eve, and Mac's mom dropped her off at Tally's house in time for dinner. Tally's parents had ordered from an Italian place not far from their home, and the girls took their baked ziti and garlic bread to the basement to watch the Maclay Finals from a couple months prior.

"This is so good," Mac said, twirling her fork to gather up the gooey cheese.

"I know, right? Wait, do you mean the food or the Maclay?"

"Both," Mac said through a mouthful of pasta and the girls laughed.

"You know what I just realized? Your name is the

beginning of Maclay. Mac-lay."

"It's a sign. I'm definitely going to be there in a few years," Mac joked, nodding at the TV.

"I'm sure you could!" Tally insisted.

"I actually do have exciting show news. It's not the Maclay, but it's still pretty amazing."

"Ooh, what is it?" Tally asked, setting her container of baked ziti down on the coffee table and settling back into the couch cross-legged.

"Ryan and I were talking about Joey's points in the division over the season and our goals for the year . . . and I think we're gonna try for Devon. We can probably qualify in just a few more shows. I've dreamed of going there since I was a short-stirrup kid. I'm going to be so nervous!"

Tally was very impressed. She'd pored over countless professional photos from Devon with all its signature baby blue and the iconic "Where Champions Meet" sign outside the Dixon Oval.

"Oh my gosh, that's amazing! I'm totally getting pictures of you jumping a fence near the champions sign."

"That's actually not part of the pony ring. The ponies go in a ring tucked back by some of the barns."

"Oh, well, then you have nothing to be nervous about," Tally joked. "We should still figure out a way to get that picture with that sign, though."

Over the next few hours, Mac and Tally watched at least a hundred Maclay rounds, streamed from Tally's laptop to the big TV in her family's basement. Mac brought pajamas to sleep over and after toasting to the New Year with sparkling cider, the girls fell asleep on a pair of air mattresses in the basement.

Two days later, on the final day of her winter

break, Tally was scheduled to hack out in the fields on Sweetie as a thank-you from the barn manager for her work. After Tally groomed and tacked the little chestnut, Brenna appeared at the stall to give her some directions.

"Hey, Tal, so you're going to want to mount up outside the school aisle and then ride up to the big paddocks on the hill," Brenna told her, as Tally pictured the area she was talking about.

"There's an old airstrip there from when private planes used to land on the property. They haven't flown in for years, so don't worry about a rogue airplane spooking your horse. Just look in between the two big paddocks up on the hill for the little walking path between them. When you get to the end of the fence line you'll see what looks like a wider grassy path. That's the old air strip. You can ride all the way up to the next property—it's a house and a small barn up in the woods. When you're parallel to those, that's when you'll want to turn around and ride back this way."

Tally nodded and thanked Brenna, feeling a shiver of excitement move through her, kind of like the way she felt when she first started taking jumping lessons. At the end of each lesson, she felt like she couldn't possibly wait until the next time she would jump.

"Oh, and once you get out to the air strip, feel free to trot and canter. The footing is pretty good out there, and thankfully dried out after the sleet, so you should be in good shape."

Tally got on Sweetie from the bench outside the barn that riders used as a mounting block. They walked up the hill and through the two paddocks until Tally could see the path open up to the air strip. As they moved closer to where the path got wider, Sweetie seemed like she might get spooky, now that they were a good distance away from all the other horses. Tally rubbed the mare's neck and she seemed to relax a bit. A few yards into the air strip, Tally noticed some brush that formed a border on each side, so she and Sweetie were traveling through a chute of sorts. The little horse was eyeing the brush, as though something might jump out at any minute. Tally was reminded of one of her favorite bits from the Maclay commentary she watched with Mac.

"It's always better to move forward," said the famous trainer doing the commentary. Tally and Sweetie may not have been in a show ring, or any ring for that matter, but the advice applied here too. The more time Sweetie had to look around and think about what scary things might be in the brush, the more likely she was to actually spook. So Tally asked her to pick up a trot.

Sweetie responded eagerly and opened her step into a big, easy trot. Tally smiled to herself, thinking about how much more relaxed the mare instantly felt. It was a unique and wonderful sensation to trot through the grass and watch the scenery go by.

After bringing the mare down to a walk for a quick breather, Tally just thought about cantering and Sweetie happily stepped into the next gait. Instead of getting strung out and heavy in the bridle during her canter, as tended to happen in lessons, Sweetie seemed to compress as they cantered along, rounding through her neck and back without Tally having to ask. She put her leg on again and felt Sweetie's stride extend as she eagerly covered the ground, her head nodding up and down as she took in the beautiful surroundings. Tally's grin was about a mile wide as they cantered up the last stretch of the hill. She felt so lucky to be in this special place, just her and Sweetie, connected in a unique and wonderful moment together outside of their usual element.

Whenever Tally sat in the back seat of her mom's car on the drive to Oaks, she'd watch the rolling hills zip by, imagining she was riding through them, feeling that surge of power as the horse cantered up the hill, the wind whipping past both their faces. And now, here she was.

It was one of the best rides she'd ever had.

After putting Sweetie away for the night and wiping down her tack, Tally went back to the mare's stall to retrieve a missing glove. Instead of standing in her usual spot munching hay, the little chestnut popped her head out over the stall guard. Sweetie only tolerated so much human time on the ground and especially in her stall, so this was an unusual gesture.

Tally scratched around the mare's ears, fluffing the hair back up where it had been matted down by the bridle. There was almost none of Sweetie's usual ear-pinning or general grumpiness, Tally noticed with a smile. They had shared a special experience on their hack out—maybe they were bonded in a new way now. Today's ride was something new for both of them, and it seemed to only deepen their trust in one another. Of all the things to love about horses, this was her favorite, Tally thought contentedly. There was always a chance to get closer to a horse.

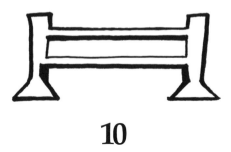

10

A couple of days later, Tally was giving Goose a once-over with her favorite soft brush when Mac joined her on the aisle.

"Hey! How's your project pony?" she asked, giving G a pat on the neck.

"He's good. Lessons on him have been so much fun, and even if he doesn't understand something he really seems to try, you know what I mean? It's just so sweet. And the first show of the Oaks series is this weekend, so we're going to do that."

"Wait, you're taking G to his very first show?"

"Well, I'm not really taking him anywhere, it's just a schooling show here at home."

"That doesn't matter!" Mac looked incredulous. "This means Ryan trusts you to give this pony a good first show experience. Like, really trusts you."

"Okay, well, I wasn't nervous about it before, but now I am. So, thanks, for that."

Mac ducked into the tack room and emerged with Joey's saddle, pads, and bridle.

"I'm coming to watch, you know."

"What? No. Why would you want to come anyway, Mac? It's a schooling show at the barn."

"So? Why do you keep saying that, anyway? I don't care where a show is; I just love showing. Don't you?"

Mac had a point, Tally thought.

"And doing it right here at home is the perfect first experience for a pony," her friend added. "Hey, I'm going to be late for this lesson and Ryan's going to kill me. I'll see you later, okay?"

Tally waved to Mac and replaced G's blanket. She made sure he was comfortable in his stall before turning her attention to the saddle she'd been borrowing. It was Isabelle's old one that she'd outgrown, and she'd been kind enough to let Tally ride in it while she tried to sell it online. As Tally conditioned the soft leather, she couldn't stop thinking about what Mac had said in regard to the upcoming show. *I don't care where a show is; I just love showing.* Tally absolutely agreed.

The Oaks schooling show series had become so popular that Brenna added a show in the first week of February to see if clients would show in the winter temperatures. Even Ryan seemed excited about the chance to give Goose an introduction to horse showing right here at home. So why was Tally being such a downer about it? She shook her head and mentally scolded herself for thinking that it was somehow less cool to do an unrated show at her own barn. She remembered having the same thought at the year-end awards and decided, right there in the tack room, to mentally take it all back. Mac's advice was spot-on—this was another chance to compete in a show. And how great was that?

A few days later, on the morning of the show, Tally was happy to wake up feeling more focused than nervous.

"Take a light feel of both sides of his mouth and keep that leg on," Ryan said from the center of the small indoor, which was being used as the schooling area. There was more commotion than usual with horses and ponies coming in and out of the ring, and a general air of excitement, but Goose didn't seem to notice.

"Good, Tal. Think about keeping the pony between your leg and your hand. Your leg moves him forward into the bridle, back to front, and your hand holds him there, just supporting lightly. Too much contact and he may take your hand too literally, right?"

Tally nodded, looking straight ahead. She'd found out the hard way in a recent lesson that a green pony could easily overreact to her body language. She was hacking G and when Ryan said something to her, she turned toward him. The shift in her weight made the pony think she wanted to turn to the inside and they nearly crashed into a jump standard. It was a startling experience for both of them. Luckily, this warm-up was going much better. Ryan set a couple of low verticals and G popped over them happily.

"Feel good? Let's go."

Tally and G followed Ryan out of the small indoor, passing the stalls used for storage at the curved end of the barn and emerging outside into the bright, sunny morning.

"I want this pony to check out his surroundings without thinking it's a big deal. Let's just walk along here and see how he does."

As they walked up the hill toward the large indoor, their breaths coming out in little white puffs suspended in the cold air, the announcer came over the loudspeaker to name the champion and reserve riders in the short stirrup division. G's head popped up and his ears pricked in the direction of the loudspeaker. Ryan clucked at him.

"Keep him moving forward," he told Tally in a soft but firm voice. Tally put both legs on the pony and noticed one gray ear flick back in her direction. That was a good sign—when a horse or pony was overly fixated on something and didn't check in with its rider, that could preface a big spook. It was promising that G was still paying attention to her. They continued up the hill and Goose exhaled loudly as he looked at his surroundings to the left and right. A group of parents lining up for coffee and hot chocolate outside of the ring seemed to interest him, but he didn't act too concerned. Tally let him check them out for a moment before encouraging him to keep walking forward.

"Good boy," Ryan said, patting G on the neck. Tally felt like a proud pony mom.

"Long stirrup riders, your division will begin

shortly, please make your way to the ring," the announcer said. The pony took only mild interest in the activity now.

"I put you in third, let's watch the first two go."

Tally and Goose were showing in the long stirrup hunter division since it was the earliest division with fences set at 2'. The ponies in the baby greens also jumped 2', but that division wouldn't go until the afternoon. Ryan wanted Goose to really experience the show atmosphere, and an earlier division was a good way to ensure that.

Tally brought G to a halt near the in-gate. He reached down to scratch his face on his left front leg, and Tally let him, holding the buckle as Ryan asked her to tell him her course. It was just a simple outside line, diagonal line, outside line. Six jumps. Plenty for the pony in his very first show atmosphere.

"He's pretty willing to do the lead change, but if he doesn't get it, make sure you do the simple. I do not want him cantering on the wrong lead around this ring."

Tally swallowed hard. She was feeling pretty good about their day so far, but Ryan's comment got the butterflies in her stomach flapping.

"Take a deep breath, Tal. We're at home. Goose doesn't seem to mind the extra activity at all. Just go in there and jump around like we do in lessons."

Tally exhaled. Ryan was right—they may have jumped this very course in their last lesson.

"And have fun." Ryan patted G on the butt and Tally steered him through the in-gate, picking up a left lead canter in the corner.

"Now on course is number 44, Tally Hart, riding Goose."

The pony skipped across the long side, his canter covering the ground effortlessly, as usual. The lines were all set at six strides. Tally thought about taking deep breaths to keep her body relaxed. She didn't want to pass along any nerves to the pony. She turned G toward the first outside line heading home and felt the first sign of his eager scoot toward the fence. Softly closing her fingers tighter around the reins, G came back to her and they met the first fence nicely. They had plenty of motor and the pony had a big stride to begin with, so Tally tried to keep everything still and quiet down the line.

Keep him between your leg and your hand. She thought of Ryan's instructions, and they met the second jump in an easy six. Jumping directly toward all the people standing along the fence line on either side of the in-gate was new for the pony and Tally

89

felt him stare at the crowd a bit. Instead of bending to the inside through the turn, G balked away from the gate a bit, as if to say, *Look at all these people! Are they here for me?*

Tally put her inside leg on harder, straightening the pony out just in time for their turn to the diagonal line. The crowd apparently no longer a concern, G agreeably bent to the inside as they turned up the diagonal. Going away from home he didn't do his little scoot so they met the first jump comfortably, and Tally sat up and closed her fingers while keeping her leg on to get out in six. Landing off the diagonal, Tally noticed that G was on his left lead. Unlike some of the other horses and ponies she'd ridden, Tally could usually feel which lead G was on, since he was so pronounced in his gait. A couple of strides before the corner, Tally stepped into her outside stirrup and looked to the right in anticipation of the turn, and G popped the cutest lead change underneath her. He sped up a little bit too, clearly proud of himself, so Tally sunk down into the tack and steadied. Coming toward home down the second outside line, she was ready for the scoot but G stayed pretty rhythmical, and she anticipated another balk at the fence line, but this time G kept his focus on her. After they'd passed the in-gate and Tally set up to turn the pony in a courtesy circle, a group of people at the gate whooped and hollered. G did a little skip-step underneath her, surprised by the reaction, but then continued along on his circle.

At the gate, Mac stood next to Ryan (Mac! Tally had almost forgotten she was here to watch) and both were beaming.

"Now that's a first horse show trip!" Ryan said, a

mint in his outstretched palm for the pony. "Tell him he's a good boy!"

Tally put the reins in her left hand and pat G on the neck, rubbing her hand all the way up toward his head and he responded with a little flip of his muzzle into the air.

"That was amazing, Tal!" Mac said on G's other side, patting the pony excitedly. Goose seemed to be enjoying all the attention and accolades. Ryan quickly reviewed Tally's second course with her. At the Oaks schooling shows, jumping classes ran straight through and were pinned before the next one started. Tally exhaled again. The pressure was off now. They had a great first trip. What was left other than to have fun and just keep riding?

"Riders, I have your results for long-stirrup hunter over fences. In first place, number 49, Scout, ridden by Kaitlyn Rowe." Tally had been so focused on getting Goose through his first horse show trip that she didn't get to watch her friend Kaitlyn go. Tally caught Kaitlyn's eye to give her a thumbs-up as one of the younger lesson kids handed her a blue ribbon.

"Second place is number 44, Goose, ridden by Tally Hart." Tally's jaw dropped open like a cartoon character. She hadn't really been thinking about how they'd pin in the class. Getting Goose around well was the priority, after all. But the red rosette that a short-stirrup rider handed her was some pretty awesome icing on the cake.

The remaining three placings were announced and Ryan told Tally he'd like her to go first in the next over fences class, so as not to give G too much time off in between. Tally nodded. It was nice not having the time to think (and stress!) about the next class. She just had to go in and ride the pony. This course was another easy six fences, starting with the other diagonal line coming home—Brenna had set the fences so that they could be jumped in either direction and there were no oxers in long stirrup. Tally walked into the ring tracking right this time, and asked Goose for his right lead canter in the corner. He sprang into the gate and Tally closed her lips around a small smile. Was G feeling proud of himself and his red ribbon?

Tally balanced the pony's canter and shaped her turn as they approached the diagonal line that they hadn't jumped yet. Goose gave the first fence a big effort, jumping in hard. Tally balanced for the six strides, knowing that he was covering the ground fast. G landed on the correct lead and Tally kept her inside leg on to keep him focused on the ring and not the spectators near the gate. They jumped up the first outside line in six strides, no problem, and then headed toward home again to jump the other outside line.

"Whoa . . ." Tally said to G softly while keeping her leg on so he wouldn't overdo it. G collected his stride just enough to meet the jump well, and Tally said "whoa" again down the line. They jumped out a tad close but it was a decent distance, Tally thought, and she immediately put her inside leg on G upon landing to keep him from balking at the crowd again. They rode through the turn and Tally's little cheering squad went wild. The second trip had felt even better than the first.

Ryan and Mac congratulated them and Ryan told Tally the second trip was an improvement.

"Just a little tight out of the second outside line,"

95

he said and Tally nodded. "But remember, these lines are set short and you've got a ton of stride. When we show somewhere off the property, you'll sit chilly and he'll get down the lines just right."

Tally was a little surprised that the mention of an away show didn't thrill her. She was too busy being happy in the moment.

"Take him for a little walk outside, but don't go far because you've got the under saddle next," Ryan said. Mac gestured to Tally and the girls walked outside with G.

"Are you so happy right now?" Mac asked.

"I'm just so . . . proud of him," Tally replied, almost feeling like she might start to cry.

"He is adorable."

The girls wandered around a bit in front of the ring, letting G drop his head to nibble on what was left of the winter grass before the announcer called for the flat. Mac produced a rag from her jeans pocket and wiped the sides of the pony's mouth.

"Ryan will be so mad if the pony has green slime coming out of its mouth in the hack," Mac said with a giggle. She wiped around G's bit before gesturing toward the ring entrance. "Go kill it!"

As the five horses and ponies trotted around the ring to start the under saddle, the announcer came back on with the results of the second over fences.

"First place goes to number 44, Goose, ridden by Tally Hart."

Tally could hardly believe her ears. They'd won. It was as if G had heard the results too, as he swished his tail and dropped his head down, trotting even cuter down the long side.

The flat class was just a happy blur for Tally, and

97

when they lined up for it to be pinned, Goose was called as the winner again. Tally smiled broadly as she accepted her second blue ribbon of the day and soaked up the announcement that Goose was champion of the long stirrup hunters. Mac snapped pictures of the two of them, and Tally was filled with satisfaction. She'd given the pony what he needed at his first show, and was bringing home a tricolor on top of that.

11

After Tally and Goose's first show together, her parents took her out for dinner at their favorite downtown restaurant to celebrate. When the dessert came out—cheesecake for Tally, cappuccinos for her parents—so did some unexpected news.

"I talked to Ryan while you were putting the pony away," her dad began. One or both of Tally's parents always stayed to watch her compete, but they made themselves scarce so as not to make her nervous. Tally always thought that was considerate of them.

"He thinks you'd really benefit from having your own saddle. He named some brands and I looked them up. They're expensive, Tal, like everything else in this sport. Even if we get one used. Mom and I talked about how much we can contribute and we'll need you to make up the rest."

"That's fine!" Tally said eagerly, happy to be working toward a nice saddle of her own.

"The Petersons across the street have asked if you'll babysit," her mom said. "Which is okay with me, as long as . . ."

"My schoolwork doesn't suffer. I know."

"Good. I'll tell Mrs. Peterson you're available."

Back at home after dinner, Tally hung a long strand of gold baker's twine that she'd found at a fabric store across one wall of her bedroom. With no window or closet on that side of her room, the wall would make the perfect canvas for her ribbons.

She scribbled the details of that day's show on the backs of the four ribbons and then put them up first. She hung the champion tricolor in the center of the twine, with the two blues and one red ribbon on either side. Then she pulled down her other favorite ribbons from above her desk to their new spot on the twine along the wall.

"It could use some more," Tally said to herself and dragged an old moving box filled with ribbons and other mementos out of her closet. Dumping them on her bed, she flipped each one over to see what she'd written. If there were meaningful ones in the box, she decided, she'd add them to the twine hung across the wall. Nothing really caught her eye until she flipped over a fourth-place rosette and read the back.

"Sweetie, Oaks schooling show, low hunter. 8 horses, OK trip. No ribbon in medal bc it SUCKED."

Tally remembered that show well. It was her first with Ryan and it was pretty much a mess. It was crazy to think about how much she'd learned in just the several months she'd been riding with him. Repacking the box, Tally pulled out a couple of blue ribbons from her very first show, along with that fourth-place ribbon with the note about the bad medal trip on the back. Then she hung all three on the twine. She might not be proud of that white rosette from her disappointing show day, but it was a great reminder of how far she'd already come, and how much room there always was to improve.

The next day was terribly cold. The forecasted high temperature was only in the low twenties, but the winds made it feel far colder. Tally had a shift at the barn after school, even though lessons had been cancelled. The horses and ponies all stayed in the night before when the temperature first dropped and the wind picked up; so Brenna devised a schedule for them to stretch their legs in brief indoor group "turnouts." They were already approaching twentyfour hours being cooped up in their stalls. Thankfully, the barn had heat lamps in place for the coldest days of the winter.

"The full-time grooms will handle hay, water, and feed this afternoon," she told Tally. "You'll follow this schedule to alternate the horses in the ring. Each group gets twenty minutes so we can make sure everyone has a chance in there. We set it up based on who gets turned out in the field together so they should get along fine. But we'll need you to keep an eye on them to make sure no one gets into trouble.

Start out by moving the rails to the wall and the standards into the corner. Kelsey is working today too, so you can clear the ring together."

Tally grabbed her winter riding gloves from her grooming box, since they'd have better grip for lifting rails and standards, and then headed to the small indoor.

"Hey," Kelsey greeted her with a smile. "Cold enough for you?"

"It's crazy! But at least there's no wind in here."

"The horses are probably getting really antsy. I'm glad they get to run around in the ring."

Tally agreed, thinking about being stuck in her room for an entire day and night. She was glad to help get the animals a change of scenery and the chance to run around and play a bit.

The girls carried the rails to the ends of the ring

and doubled up on the standards to haul them into the corners together. They laughed and joked about how synchronized they'd become and then Kelsey pulled out the list of horses to be turned out in the ring.

"Looks like we're starting with the school ponies. Lil Bit, KD, Lou Lou and Janie are going first—the four mares on the inside aisle."

"Got it," said Tally. "I'll grab Lil and KD if you want to get the other two."

Kelsey set the alarm on her phone to ring every twenty minutes so the girls knew to switch out the horses. It was fun to watch them figure out what they were doing in the indoor with no riders or tack, or even a longe line. Once they realized they didn't have to stand at the gate with Tally and Kelsey they'd either prance away or take off bucking, sometimes dropping down to roll in the footing. Brenna asked Kelsey to walk down both aisles and make sure every horse had at least its heavyweight blanket on (some of the horses required double blankets) while Tally kept an eye on the horses in the ring to make sure no one did anything too silly that could result in an injury. When a group of school horse geldings was in the ring, Scout somehow caught a hoof in his blanket strap while rolling and spooked himself, ultimately breaking the strap. Tally texted Brenna, who made a temporary replacement strap out of bailing twine, tying off the ends in complicated-looking knots.

"Glad you were watching, Tal," she said.

Tally spent the rest of her shift leading horses to and from the small indoor, and chasing down the ones who didn't want their mini-turnout to end. Others proudly checked themselves out in the arena mirrors as if they'd never seen their reflections before. Tally ended up working an hour later than usual and when her mom picked her up, she looked concerned.

"Tal, are you going to have time for your homework?"

"Of course, Mom, don't worry," Tally rushed to reassure her. A text from Isabelle came through on her phone. It turned out she was willing to sell her old saddle directly to Tally, provided Ryan thought it fit her well enough. Tally calculated how many hours of babysitting she would need to afford it with the deal Isabelle would be giving her, but she couldn't do the calculation in her head. Her mom may have had a point about that math homework.

Around eleven that night, Tally woke with a start. She was surrounded by textbooks and notes on her bed and her brain felt foggy as she tried to piece together when she'd fallen asleep. Right after getting home from the barn she told her mom she'd warm up leftovers for dinner, but had actually just brought a granola bar and a protein shake up to her room. It had been close to seven at that point, and the empty shake bottle now sat at the top of her trash can. From the looks of her homework, she hadn't made much headway. Still trying to remember the sequence of events that evening, Tally was startled by a knock on the door. It opened slowly and her dad slipped inside her room.

"I came in to see how you were doing at around eight o'clock, and you were sound asleep," he whispered with a laugh. "Long day at the barn, huh?"

"Yeah, we had to turn the horses out in the ring and . . . I'll get my homework done, don't worry."

"I'm not. And I won't tell Mom, either, as long as that homework really does get done and your grades don't slip. You know I love to see you working so hard at your sport."

"Thanks, Dad. Night."

"Night, Tal."

12

For one of Tally's lessons on Goose soon after their show, Ryan added more flower boxes and filler to the jumps in the large indoor. He also set up a second pair of standards to the outs of the lines to make them oxers. Guess it's time to step things up, Tally thought to herself.

"Come on over here a minute," Ryan said after Tally had walked Goose around the ring on a loose rein. "Stand up in two point . . . now sit." He eyed Isabelle's old saddle carefully. "I think this saddle fits you well now, and will keep fitting you if you grow another couple inches. See how you've got some more room here?" He pointed to the few inches of saddle flap Tally had in front of her knees.

"Just try not to shoot up to like, five foot nine, okay?"

"I'll do my best," Tally said with a laugh.

"If the price works out and you want to buy this saddle from Isabelle, I think it's as good an option as any. If we take some saddles out on trial, that's gonna be time-consuming, and you may end up paying more, too. We know this saddle fits you and Goose, and it should fit other ponies and potentially horses, too. And when you get too tall for it, you can sell it and buy a new one. Isabelle bought it new and didn't have it long before she outgrew it, so it's in great shape."

"Sounds good. Thank you, Ryan."

He gave her a thumbs-up before asking her to start trotting around, working on some circles with the pony as he finished setting jumps. For the flatwork part of their lesson, Tally worked on lengthening and shortening Goose's stride at the trot and canter. It took a lot of leg to keep him moving in the gait that she wanted while maintaining the collection. The answer to most questions while riding, it seemed, was to add leg.

When it was time to start jumping, Ryan had them warm up over ground rails set in a five-stride line, and then he made the second rail a small vertical.

"There's an actual jump now, so you'll need to keep him collected, just like we did on the flat, to fit in your five strides."

Tally cantered the rail and then collected. But G

had too much stride and took off from a long spot after just four strides.

"Stop, stop, stop. What happened there?"

"I didn't collect enough?"

"You didn't collect soon enough," Ryan said. "Think about compressing that canter stride on your approach to the rail. You just rode it the same way as when it was two rails. You're not going to have the time in the middle of the line to collect enough. Try it again and get that shorter stride, that bouncy canter, before you're even approaching the rail. Create that canter you want before you even approach the line."

Duh, Tally thought, why didn't I think of that? Sometimes she just felt so eager to be jumping that she made dumb mistakes like this one. Luckily, she also felt like she always had a clean slate with Ryan to try something again after making a mistake.

The next time around she thought about compressing G's stride early and keeping that more collected canter down the short side and through the turn to the line. The pony made a solid effort jumping in, even though it was just a rail, but Tally was able to hold the collected canter and they jumped out in five.

"Well done. One more time."

After another successful line in five strides, Ryan set a full course for Tally and Goose—to challenge the pony a bit, he said. He explained that the home show had gone so well that he felt confident in pushing the pony to step outside its comfort zone and gain more confidence.

As Tally was memorizing the course Ryan mapped out for her, she felt G balk at something next to one of the jump standards. It was a jacket lined with a metallic silver fabric, left behind by another rider. She urged G forward to let him check it out.

"It's more important that the pony is paying attention to you, Tal, than getting him to go sniff whatever is spooking him. Let's put him on a circle here where he has to pass the scary jacket. Keep him bent to the inside and listening to you, not paying attention to what he's afraid of." After a couple of circles at the walk, Tally asked G to trot, correcting him when he tried to come out of his inside bend to look at the jacket again.

"Okay, now go get the full course," said Ryan.

Tally picked up the canter and focused on a medium pace for the pony. Her course started with the single vertical on the diagonal, outside line, diagonal line, outside line. Flowers, filler, and oxers in the lines gave the course a more daunting appearance than the plain verticals they'd jumped just a couple days ago in the schooling show. Approaching the first jump, Tally felt Goose lock in on it but kept her leg on to ride through. He was staring at the jacket again. The pony sucked back as if he wanted to stop but Tally legged him hard and clucked. Goose chipped spectacularly and Tally tried her best to stay with him but ultimately got left behind the motion. She regained her balance a couple strides after the jump.

"Ride him through that turn and then stop," Ryan said. Tally immediately thought back to the drive-by that Danny pulled at their first and only show (make that their first and only jump at the show) together.

"Take a deep breath," Ryan said. "You got him over the jump and that's what matters for that first attempt. Now he knows he can do it, so let's see if you can finesse it this time. Jump that single by itself again and halt straight. If he's more agreeable about it this time, give him a big pat and tell him he's a good boy. Make a big deal about it so he feels proud of himself."

Tally rode up to the vertical—and the scary jacket—with her leg on tight, ready to kick if the pony sucked back. But this time he maintained an even pace. A stride before the jump he swapped his lead, but he cleared the fence without much drama, so Tally halted straight and pet him.

"Did you feel him swap?"

"Yes."

"Do you know why he did that?"

"Um, no."

"Because he wasn't straight. He's still a little focused on that jacket so he got squirrely and over-bent to the inside. Make a circle here and continue on with your

117

course. We don't need to tie him up in knots about this one jump. Keep going with the rest."

Tally circled and picked up her left lead canter to head to the outside line. Goose felt much more civilized now, with no silver-lined outerwear in sight, and made big, but manageable efforts over the vertical, then five strides to the oxer out.

"Good! Now sit up through the turn and balance, keep your pace the same as you jump up the diagonal line."

The jumps were noticeably bigger and had a lot more filler than at the show, but Tally was pleasantly surprised to find that G jumped them almost the same. He made a little more effort, and it was fun to catch some air over the jumps, but she made sure to hold her body up and not revert to her old habit of exuberantly laying down on the neck.

Down the next outside line, G continued to canter steadily along, and when they landed off the oxer, Ryan told her to continue on and catch the first jump of the course again—the spooky jacket vertical.

"Don't overthink it. Just keep things flowing like you have been. Keep him straight and steady."

Fighting the urge to think about it too much—Tally was quite good at that, she'd realized—she rode down to the single vertical like it was any of the other six jumps they'd cleared with ease. And the pony seemed to sense her calm assertiveness; they met it straight, with no swap, and cantered away to finish the course.

"Nice, Tal! Give him a big pat, tell him he's a good boy."

Tally patted G on both sides of his neck and told him what a good pony he was—and so brave jumping the fence with the jacket.

They did the course once more, doubling up on the spooky single again before the lesson was over.

"So, next week I'm taking a few kids to a local A just a few miles from here. Low-stress, but great mileage for the pony. Would you want to show Goose for me?"

"I'd love to but . . . you think I can do it?"

"Why wouldn't you be able to?"

"I just mean what happened last time, with Danny and all."

"Tally," Ryan said, resting his arm behind the saddle and giving G a pat. "We've been through this. That was another time, another pony, another situation entirely. You have to be able to put that out of your head."

"I guess I just feel like I can put in a decent round

here at home but what if I can't do it at a show somewhere else?"

"Based on what? One naughty pony who—as we found out the hard way—needed more schooling? This is a totally different animal. Literally. I wouldn't ask you if I didn't think you could do it, Tal."

"Okay. I'm in."

"Good. I'll get you the information. Goose is a sales pony and you're my catch rider on him, so I won't charge you for the shows, just your weekly lessons as we've been doing. That work for you?"

"Yes. Thank you, Ryan!"

"Thank you, Tal. Try not to stress. It's the same stuff we've been doing, just in a different location."

That night, Tally had a babysitting job at the Petersons' house. They had a three-year-old and a five-year-old, both of whom were asleep by the time

Tally got there at 7:30 p.m. She'd gotten about fifteen minutes into her English homework when Mac called.

The girls chatted about Mac's recent show on Joey, and Tally found herself getting excited on her friend's behalf for Devon. She was hoping her parents would let her go with Mac to watch.

"It's like a whole new world, not chipping at shows. We went to a one-day show over the weekend and we were reserve champion again."

"That's awesome!"

"Thanks. It's just nice to feel like we have some consistency, you know?"

One of the Peterson kids came downstairs for a glass of water, so Tally ended her call and got her little charge back to bed. Then she sat on the couch with the rest of her math homework.

Once finished, she rewarded herself by watching pony rounds from Devon the year before, daydreaming for her friend. And maybe for herself, too. Someday.

13

Tally's first show with Goose off the property was held at a barn called Rose Ridge, not far from Oaks. It was a relatively small facility, but known for putting on some of the nicest two-day rated shows in the area. They also had homemade pie at the food stand that everyone raved about.

"Pie is for winners," she'd heard Ryan joke with Isabelle recently. "Guess I'll have to win a class, then," she joked back.

Tally had heard about this particular show venue more than once from Mac, and she was excited to explore the grounds with her friend and watch some of the earlier divisions. Tally was only showing on Sunday, but Mac had also competed the day before. It went really well for them, too, with Joey earning a second place in his first over fences trip, and winning the under saddle.

In order to preserve Goose's green eligibility, Tally would be showing him in the children's pony division. A pony like Goose could potentially be more marketable if you sold him as an eligible green, Ryan had explained to her. Ponies only had a year to compete in their green division before moving on to the regular ponies. So competing Goose in a C-rated division, like the children's ponies, would keep him eligible to compete as a small green pony with whoever bought him. Tally didn't like to think about G getting sold, but Ryan said it wouldn't be a possibility until August at the earliest. In the mean-time, it felt really special to be a part of the pony's education.

The regular pony divisions went first that Sunday morning, so the girls were there by seven. Tally and Mac stood along the fence line in the indoor ring watching the small ponies go.

"I've never seen so many giant bows in one place," Tally whispered to Mac.

"Yeah, some people are really into those," Mac replied with a nod toward one tiny girl on a paint pony, her braids and bows bouncing dramatically above her number. "They're cute on little kids but they can be a little distracting, too. Oh, wait, you have to see this pony go."

Tally didn't need to ask Mac which pony she was talking about. It was obvious to her, and most other people watching in the indoor. Entering the ring was an eye-catching palomino pony. Tally couldn't help but giggle. He had the most dramatic trot she'd ever seen, and an air about him like he considered himself to be the single biggest star of the show.

"That's Pineapple," Mac said.

"He's . . . a showman!"

"You can say that again."

The girls watched as the little palomino jumped around, hiking his knees up high over each jump and earning a boisterous round of applause from the spectators.

"He's actually got his own social media following," Mac said.

"The pony does?"

"Yeah, he's such a character."

Tally watched as Pineapple pranced a bit around

the in-gate, obviously feeling good about himself after his round.

After they watched a few more smalls, Ryan came over and said it was time for Mac to get on her pony. Tally's lessons hadn't been lining up with her friend's lately, so she was eager to see how she and Joey were doing. Both looked very businesslike in the warm-up ring, Tally noticed, and Mac appeared to be more confident than before. Today they had their second over fences class and then the handy round, in which a rider showed off his or her pony's handiness with things like trot jumps and rollback turns.

"Think about keeping that consistent rhythm," Tally heard Ryan tell Mac as they walked to the indoor ring. "Use the corners to slow down if you need to."

"In for their second hunter trip, number 308,

Smoke Hill Jet Set, ridden by Mackenzie Bennett."

Mac had her usual steely expression on her face, and an air of calm determination as she guided Joey into the ring. Tally remembered that look from the first time she saw Mac riding at Oaks. She'd admired it ever since. As Mac piloted Joey around the jumps, Tally was impressed. She'd always looked up to Mac as a rider but the pair had made obvious improvements since the last time Tally saw them show. Joey covered the ground between the fences with ease, and Mac sat up straight in the saddle on her approaches, looking coolly confident that they'd meet the jumps just right. And they did.

Standing next to Ryan as Mac jumped around, she heard him say "whoa" as the pony approached the corners. Tally noticed that Joey could get a little strong landing off the lines, but Mac somehow made it look invisible when she got him back to his steady rhythm.

The first course looked great to Tally, as did their handy round, in which Mac made a slick inside turn and Joey met the jumps perfectly out of stride. Tally wasn't surprised when they were called back to jog second in the first over fences, and then jogged first in the handy.

"That handy is becoming your specialty," Ryan said to Mac, giving her a high five as she exited the ring. Joey looked so proud with a blue ribbon hooked on his bridle.

"He makes it really fun," Mac said, giving Joey a pat. Their two second places and two firsts made them champion of the division.

Ryan had a private little conference with Mac outside of the ring, his hand on top of her helmet as he spoke, before giving her a big hug and unwrapping a peppermint for Joey. Lupe replaced Joey's bridle with his padded shipping halter, and Tally joined Mac to walk back to the trailer.

"We have to take pictures!" Tally said, pulling both Mac and Joey in for a hug.

"Yes! I still can't believe it. We've never been champion before. Guess all those tough lessons paid off!"

The girls laughed and chatted on the walk back to the trailer. As they got closer, Pineapple's rider, who was letting the pony graze in the field where the trailers parked, gave them a wave.

"Congratulations," she said, nodding to the championship ribbon Mac had hooked onto her jacket pocket. "We should take a picture together."

"Sure!" Mac said, leading Joey over. Pineapple arched his neck and almost appeared to be sizing up the larger chestnut pony. Then he let out a high-pitched whinny.

"Oh, don't mind him," Pineapple's rider said with a roll of her eyes. "He's the most competitive pony on the planet." She turned to the little palomino: "You're still special, don't worry."

Someone came off the trailer to hand her the small pony championship ribbon and congratulated Mac and Joey on their medium championship.

"I'll take the picture for you," the woman said, and the girls posed with their ponies, the blue, red, and yellow ribbons waving slightly in the breeze on the ponies' halters.

"Do you have a mint wrapper or anything to crinkle?" the woman asked Tally. "That'll get their attention to put their ears forward," Mac added. Tally was grateful for her friend, who always seemed to know when Tally could use a new little horse show lesson.

Once all four ears were pricked and the photo shoot was successful, Mac let Joey graze outside the Field Ridge trailer. Tally's classes would be starting soon, so she went to the trailer dressing room to put on her boots and her helmet. She'd been wearing tall boots and putting her hair up into her helmet for a least a year now, but she couldn't help but wonder if she should be fitting in more with all the paddock boots and bows she saw at the show. She made a mental note to ask Mac about it.

Soon, Tally was warming up Goose on the flat in the schooling ring. The pony was definitely more animated and distracted than he'd been at their home show, but Ryan assured her this was normal and told her to continue calmly getting G's attention back. Tally herself was a tad distracted by how cute he looked braided, but she reminded herself to keep her eyes up as she rode. After cantering a couple of laps, and making circles when the traffic in the schooling area allowed, Ryan told Tally to walk G while he claimed a schooling jump for them and set it as a cross-rail to start.

"Think about nothing but keeping this pony straight," Ryan told her as Goose looked left and right at all the activity.

"Circle again. Inside bend. Overdo it if you have to. He has to pay attention to you, Tal."

After their circle, Goose felt rounder through his back, and Tally kept contact evenly through both legs and both hands to keep him from swapping in front of the jump.

"Three, two, one, that's the ride. Do it again."

After a couple more cross-rails, then verticals, it was time to go into the ring. Tally could feel herself starting to think too hard about what was ahead of them.

"Eight jumps. Nothing else. Think about nothing else," Ryan told her with a wink.

Tally didn't hear their names announced as they walked into the ring. She couldn't even remember her number. This wasn't the time to soak in the show atmosphere or think about ribbons or anything like that. All she had to do was pilot Goose over eight jumps.

The first fence was a single vertical on the diagonal, much like they'd been doing in their most recent lesson. Goose was a little wiggly on the approach and swapped in front of it, but he made a nice round effort over the jump. Going away, Tally focused on their straightness and G changed his lead effortlessly. Next was an outside line with bright pink flowers and G definitely peeked at them a little bit in the air, jumping high up over the vertical. He coasted down the line in six strides and jumped the oxer nicely, without a peek this time. The rest of the course brought much of the same. A swap here, a counter-bend there. But no glaring errors, and when they landed off the final jump, Tally couldn't help but smile. Goose tried so hard for her and had a successful first trip at a big show.

"Well done, Tally, I'm proud of you both," Ryan said as they left the ring. "I think you're riding just a tad too tentative. Remember your lesson the other day and think about the pony's straightness. If he's impressed with a jump and peeks at it, there's nothing we can do. And it's appropriate for a green pony. But I think you can ride through those wiggles better, and then he won't swap. Overall, though, really good. I hope you're proud of yourself, too."

Tally felt her cheeks turn red but she didn't even mind. The first course felt solid and she was excited to see if they could improve on it.

When Ryan led Goose up to the in-gate for their next trip, Tally took a deep breath and tried to recreate the feelings from the lesson when they worked so hard on straightness. Their second course started out better, with no swaps and a straighter pony. They approached the diagonal line a little too quietly and got a bit close to the vertical going in, but Tally was able to move Goose up to get the strides and not have to add. The same thing happened down the final outside line, with a tighter distance in, but Tally rode up to get the strides coming out.

Walking out of the ring, Ryan and Mac were both clapping loudly alongside Isabelle, who'd joined them at the fence line.

"Not bad at all, Tal, just a couple of tight spots coming in. Do you know why that happened?"

"I . . . it's all kind of a blur, I'm sorry."

"That's okay. You were super focused on keeping him straight, which is just what I wanted, but in doing that you took some of his step away and changed the rhythm, which is why you got in tight. But the fact that you were able to just close your leg and get out without adding was impressive! The whole course was straighter than the first and he didn't swap, so that's great. I'm really proud of you, kiddo."

Tally dismounted and gave G a big hug. With just two classes, their show day was done. The other half of the division had gone the day before, but Ryan thought one day would be plenty for the pony's first big rated show. Lupe took Goose from Tally, and Ryan congratulated her again before heading off to get Isabelle and her horse warmed up for their division.

"Want to watch the rest of the class and wait for your ribbons?" Mac asked her with a big smile.

"You . . . you think we'll get ribbons?"

Mac threw her head back, laughing. "Of course! You guys were awesome and Goose is easily the cutest pony so far."

The girls stood along the rail and watched another half dozen ponies go. Tally thought back on Goose's great show attitude, and she felt proud to be his rider, and she felt proud to be his rider. As for the other ponies in the class, some added down the lines, one had a stop, and others put in solid-looking trips. Tally didn't know how she and G stacked up but she surprised herself by not actually caring how they'd pin. And that was an awesome feeling.

After the last pony left the ring, the jump crew went to work adjusting the fences for the next division. Tally noticed a posted order-of-go near the ring for all the classes. There were fifteen ponies in her division. Was Mac right? Would she and G pin at all in this big group?

When the announcer's voice came on the PA, Tally couldn't help holding her breath, hoping to hear Goose's name. But it was Mac who recognized Tally's number first. She squealed with excitement and Tally couldn't hear what the announcer said.

"What?" she asked Mac, who was now jumping up and down.

"You were fifth in the first class, Tal!" Mac ran off

to find Tally's ribbon and Tally listened in disbelief as they announced the results of the second class.

"Third place is number 324, Goose, ridden by Tally Hart."

Third place out of fifteen ponies in a big rated show. And on her sweet little greenie! Tally couldn't stop smiling, and Mac returned with the ruffly pink and yellow rosettes.

"Congrats, catch rider," Mac said, hooking a ribbon on each of Tally's pockets. Tally knew exactly what she and Mac should do next.

"Thanks. Now let's go get some pie!"

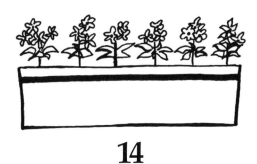

14

As winter turned to spring that year, riders were shedding their extra layers of clothing as horses shed their winter coats. The buzz of clippers could be heard up and down the aisles as the particularly fuzzy horses and ponies got a fresh cut for the new season. Tally had been babysitting throughout the winter and, with some help from her parents, earned enough to buy Isabelle's old saddle. Her parents had written a check to Isabelle's parents, and Isabelle popped off the gold nameplate on the back of the saddle so Tally could add her own. She planned to pick up the one she'd ordered at the tack shop after her shift.

Tally spent the first hour of her shift on the first truly warm spring day by helping Brenna set jumps in the large indoor. There was an Oaks schooling show planned for the following day. Tally and Brenna went into a musty closet to retrieve the flower boxes reserved only for shows—it was the best way to ensure they'd stay in decent shape. Tally replaced the flowers that had fallen out, sticking the green ends into the holes and fluffing up the blooms before placing the boxes at each jump.

"Tal, if you could set each jump as an eighteen-inch vertical, that would be great. Make sure there's a flower box or wall on either side of each jump. The courses are set to jump everything in both directions. And that'll be it for your shift today," Brenna said. "Thanks so much for your help. Are you showing tomorrow?"

"I wish I could, but I have to go away with my parents for a wedding out of town."

"Next time!" Brenna said brightly on her way out of the ring. She passed Mac, who was on her way in to see Tally.

"Hey! Need a hand?"

"Sure," Tally said, pointing her finger as she counted how many boxes and walls (unadorned flower boxes painted to look like brick walls) she had left to fill the jumps.

"We're supposed to set a single rail at eighteen inches so the jumps are ready for the first class of the day. I think that's the first hole on these standards."

"Got it," said Mac, readjusting her sweaty ponytail. "How is it suddenly, like, summer?"

"I don't know, but it's better than being cold!"

"I guess, but the weather means we're getting close

to Devon and I'm not *reaaaaady*."

"Of course you're ready, what do you mean?"

"I guess it's just a lot of pressure. I've wanted to go to Devon forever, but . . . I don't know. I probably shouldn't have any expectations."

"Well, I'm still pretty new at this, but when I was daydreaming about ribbons on Danny, I fell off at the first jump. When I focused on nothing but getting around and having a smooth course, I pinned well with Goose."

"No, you're right. It's so true. I can't have any expectations but to have fun and do our best." Mac settled a rail into the jump cups and followed Tally to the middle of the ring to get the next set of flower boxes. "Plus, there's all the great food and the fair, so it's going to be really fun no matter what. Did your parents say you can come?"

Tally had been talking about Devon with her mom and dad for weeks now, but they hadn't officially given her the green light to travel with Mac. She felt a trickle of sweat slide down her back as she lugged the heavy wall to the vertical near the judges' box.

"I think they will."

"Good. We're going to have so much fun!"

Half an hour and dozens of boxes and rails later, Tally and Mac stood back by the in-gate to admire their work in the ring. All the jumps looked uniform and the boxes made for much prettier ground lines than the usual spare rail at the base of the standards.

"Outside, diagonal, outside, single. Go!" Mac said, taking off at the human version of the canter toward the first jump. Tally followed her, laughing as they counted their own strides down what would be a five-stride line for horses. Mac got twelve and Tally got eleven.

"Don't cut your turn!" Mac yelled as Tally cantered ahead of her down the short side of the ring toward their next line.

"If I stay out, this . . . will take all day," Tally shouted back between gulps of air, her stomach muscles tight from the effort and from laughing. They lost count down the diagonal line and Tally broke to a trot in front of the outside line, breathing hard.

"Automatic 55!" Mac shouted as the girls bumbled down their last jumps.

Panting and still laughing at the end of their course, Tally and Mac ambled out of the ring and down to the barn, fishing change out of their pockets for the soda machine.

"Just don't do the course like that," Tally said, nodding her head in the direction of the big indoor, "and you'll be fine." The girls sat down on the

147

bleachers and Mac giggled in response. "Hey, so what did you mean about 'automatic 55?' "

Mac took a long sip of her drink and blinked hard, as if trying to remember.

"Oh, you mean for trotting on course? That's the automatic score you get. A refusal is an automatic 40. If you add down a line it's like, low 60s. Stuff like that."

"I didn't even realize rounds got a numbered score like that." Tally was well past feeling embarrassed with Mac. She actually really liked learning more about showing through her friend.

"Yeah, they don't always announce them. Only in certain classes and at the really big shows where you have to qualify."

"What's the highest score you've ever gotten?"

Mac looked thoughtful again. "I think Joey's gotten

an 84 or an 85. He'd probably do better if I wasn't getting in his way."

Tally swatted Mac with a rag that someone had left on the bleachers.

"Weren't you champion just a few weeks ago?"

"I just want to make everyone proud at Devon, you know? I don't want to leave feeling like I could have done better."

Tally understood that completely.

"Oh, I almost forgot, I get to pick up my nameplate today!"

Mac followed Tally as she climbed down from the bleachers and out into the parking lot. The tack shop was situated just outside the barn. The girls walked into the store, where the cool air from the window AC unit made the small space feel amazing.

After careful consideration, Tally had decided on

large block print for her nameplate and ordered it a couple of weeks prior. It might have been silly to be this excited about something so small, but having only ridden in school saddles and those borrowed from other riders, it was special to finally have her own.

"We can attach it for you here if you'd like," the woman behind the register said. Mac offered to go grab the saddle from the boarders' tack room and Tally thanked her, taking a few minutes to browse the grooming aisle. She felt her cheeks color as she remembered her embarrassing elbow-grease moment in the tack store, but that also felt like ancient history now. She laughed at herself a little bit for having thought that elbow grease was an actual product, and not just an expression for putting a lot of work—day in and day out—into grooming your horse.

Mac returned with Tally's saddle and the

saleswoman took it to the back room to attach the nameplate with tiny gold nails. She returned and showed it to Tally, who beamed in response.

"TALLY HART" looked just right on the back of the saddle.

151

15

"I cannot believe I am packing my trunk for Devon." Mac shook her head as Tally helped her roll a final pair of clean black polo wraps.

Tally smiled at her friend. It was a pretty amazing accomplishment, especially considering how down in the dumps Mac had been about her partnership with Joey when the pair first arrived at Oaks.

"Do you have any good luck charms that you'll wear, or keep in your jacket pocket or something?" Tally asked.

"Well, I always show with a tail bracelet from my first pony. But I'm not sure I have anything else that's lucky," Mac said. "If we don't forget anything in this tack trunk, that will be lucky. Maybe a miracle," she added with a laugh. "I can't tell you how many times Ryan has asked me for something at a show and I didn't bring it."

Tally looked at everything packed so far inside Mac's trunk: two extra bits; eight polos total; three sets of spurs—tiny nubs, and two pairs with roller balls; Joey's leather show girth; a trio of sparkly white show pads; longe line and whip; a bucket of exceptionally clean brushes; a currycomb; and a hoof pick.

"What's left on the list?" she asked her friend.

"Clean rags for Joey and for my boots, plus Joey's sheets," Mac said. "They're in the dryer now. I'll go grab them."

When Mac returned to the tack room with the sheets and rags, neatly folded and piled, Tally surveyed the trunk contents once more.

"Okay, so what are you forgetting?"

Mac closed her eyes for a moment, thinking hard.

"My show bat!" she announced triumphantly.

"You can't just use your regular crop?" Tally asked.

"It's my little tradition," Mac said, pulling a bat from her backpack and tucking it under the saddle pads in her trunk. "When I had a naughty short stirrup pony I started carrying it because it's heavier—it reminds me that I can use it if I need to!"

"Did you have to use it when you showed that pony?"

"Oh, all the time," Mac said with a laugh. "He could be a real brat. Joey shouldn't need it, but Ryan says you always carry one, just in case. And I guess it's sort of a show tradition that I carry this particular bat. I'd feel weird without it. Okay, let's go see Joey before they load him onto the trailer. Oh my gosh, this is so real now!"

Mac followed her friend out to the parking lot where the smaller Field Ridge trailer was parked. There was already a big bay horse loaded inside, peeking out its window.

"Who is that?" Tally asked.

"That's Pip," Mac said. "He's Isabelle's junior hunter, the one who lives at the end of the aisle."

"Oh, right. Good luck, sweet boy!" Tally said to the horse on the trailer, and both girls turned when they heard a little whinny.

Just outside the barn, Lupe was leading Joey toward the trailer.

"Aw, my boy!" Mac jogged over to her pony, who nodded his head toward Pip on the trailer. He looked ready to go in his padded shipping halter, boots, and cooler. Mac gave him a big hug around his neck.

"Trunk packed, Mac Attack?" Lupe asked her with a wink.

"All packed," Mac said. "Even my show bat."

"Thank goodness for that," Lupe joked back. "Okay, boy, let's go."

Both girls watched as Joey climbed up the ramp and Lupe secured him inside.

"Safe trip, buddy," Mac called. Filled with excitement for her friend, Tally wrapped her up in a hug.

Next stop: Devon.

16

Tally woke up abruptly from a dream and looked around the dark room. It wasn't her room. Where was she? Then it all came back to her in a rush. She was in a hotel room with Mac and Mac's mom, just outside of the show grounds in Devon, Pennsylvania. Tally's mom hadn't let her come to see her friend's first day of showing since it was a Friday and Tally had school. But they made the trip right after school let out that afternoon; Tally was excited to join her friend, but sad to learn that Mac was very disappointed with how the show had gone thus far.

Mac and Joey had two jumping classes the first day of Devon, and they did not go as planned. Their first trip, the small pony hunter conformation class, went okay. They'd scored a 74 for having some bobbles here and there, and ended up right in the middle of the pack, fifteenth place out of thirty in the class. Ryan told Mac that he knew she could ride better than that. But their next trip, a regular over fences class, was a total disaster.

Mac texted Tally shortly after the class and said that she really psyched herself out, having so many family members in attendance to watch her show, and their trip was a mess. She started out too slow and they chipped at the first jump. Then she moved Joey up to get a better pace going and they went past the distance to the two-stride, ending up with another big chip going in. Since Joey jumped in weak, he had a lot of ground to make up in just the two strides. Mac legged him hard to get the two, but she also threw her body ahead of the motion and Joey had to add another awkward half-stride before jumping out. Mac lost a stirrup in the process and could barely remember the rest of the trip, just that they barely got around and scored a 50. The pair ended up twenty-eighth out of thirty in the class, and Mac left the ring in tears.

The girls had decided to get ice cream together in the hotel restaurant that night.

"Everybody has bad trips from time to time. I think you told me that," Tally said, hoping to cheer her friend up.

"I know. But this was probably my worst trip ever. And it happened at Devon of all places. Everyone

159

was watching and I was so embarrassed."

Tally took a bite of her DIY sundae and thought a moment. "Yeah, but your relatives aren't horse people. I'm sure they didn't even know you made mistakes. What did Ryan say?"

"He was really nice about it. He was like, 'It's okay to be upset, but let's keep moving forward. We need to figure out what went wrong and fix it.' The good thing is we love the handy and that's tomorrow."

"Just bring that confidence to the handy," Ryan chimed in. He'd heard the end of the girls' conversation while walking up to their table in the hotel restaurant. "Mac, you're kinda like Tom Brady. Just when you think he's down and out, he comes back. It's almost easier this way. You can only do better than you did today. Get some sleep tonight, girls, we've got an early start in the morning."

As Tally lay in the unfamiliar hotel bed late that night, she heard Mac shift positions before settling back in under the covers of her own bed. Mac's mom was on the pull-out couch, snoring softly. As Tally drifted off to sleep, she made a wish that her friend would have a better third day at the show. Mac and Joey had worked hard and she wanted them to leave Devon happy.

"Rise and shine, sleepy heads!" Mac's mom turned on the light on the nightstand between the girls' beds, and Tally squinted at the clock radio: 6:00 a.m. Mac bumbled into the bathroom while Tally hung her upper body out of the bed to dig through her duffle bag on the floor. She pulled out a pair of jean shorts, a tank top, and a hoodie, and changed into them under the sheets—a skill honed during the overnight horse camp she'd attended a few summers ago.

"The car is already loaded with all your show stuff, Mackenzie. Just pop on your breeches and show shirt and we'll be good to go. The lobby has bagels and coffee so we can grab those on the way out."

"Thanks, Mom," Mac mumbled and stepped out of the bathroom to grab her clothes from the closet, then went back in to change.

"I hope today goes better for her," Mac's mom whispered to Tally once her daughter had closed the door. "I'm worried we put too much pressure on her yesterday. Her grandparents and her aunt and uncle only live an hour away so it seemed like a good chance for them to watch her ride."

"Ryan gave her a good pep talk last night. I think it'll go better," Tally said, trying to sound optimistic for Mac's mom.

Just after 7 a.m., they pulled up to the show grounds. The sign greeted them as they parked: "Devon Horse Show & Country Fair." In the early morning light, the Devon blue that adorned so many of the surfaces made the whole place look soft and inviting. The fairgrounds lay dormant, as it was too early for any of the rides or games to be operating, but the fair itself gave the horse show a totally unique feel. It was set up directly in front of the entrance and the show rings were off to the right. Tally was surprised by how much smaller and more compact the grounds were in person than they appeared in photos and video. The fair was practically right on top of the horse show!

The Dixon Oval itself, however, was huge, and Tally listened in as the riders in front of her talked about how difficult it can be to compete in. "Like

163

riding in a big blue bowl," she heard one of the girls say.

Tally, Mac, and Mac's mom, Cindy, walked down the long side of the ring, and Tally caught herself staring at some of the junior hunters flatting around. They were absolutely stunning. It was almost like catching a glimpse of real, live unicorns. Mac and her mom made a left-hand turn at the end of the ring (right past the "Where Champions Meet" sign!) to walk around to the Wheeler Ring, where the ponies would compete—just past a small schooling area in between the two show rings. The grounds were punctuated by spires atop the buildings and the Devon blue was everywhere. It was almost like they were walking through a baby blue postcard.

Lupe stood with Joey just outside the schooling ring. Mac took her helmet, gloves, and crop out of her backpack and put everything on to ride. Lupe gave her a leg up and off they went to walk around the schooling area as they waited to school.

"Morning, Cindy. Morning, Tal," Ryan said upon joining them. "I'm going to hack her around, and then we can grab coffees and talk strategy for the morning, okay?"

Tally watched as Ryan signaled for Mac to join him in the middle of the ring. He spoke to her for a bit before giving the pony an affectionate smack on the behind and sending them out to the rail. Whatever he said must have worked because Joey flatted great, and Tally saw Mac smile here and there. It was impossible to make out what Ryan was saying in the busy ring, but Tally was glad Mac seemed to be in a better mood this morning.

After handing Joey off to Lupe, the group headed

over to get drinks and talk.

They sat under an umbrella at a table for four—it was already quite warm for being so early in the morning. Ryan told Mac to forget about yesterday as best as she could and just focus on having a solid round today.

"It didn't even happen. Okay? Horse showing is supposed to be fun. Particularly this show! So take it all in a bit while you're watching the smalls go and try to enjoy yourself. Then when you get on, you'll jump that handy course just like we do at home and at the shows. You've got this. Just get up to ring pace. That's all I want you to think about."

Mac nodded and Tally noticed the confidence seemed to have returned to her face. Mac's mom looked a bit relieved as well.

"I'll meet you girls at the ring in twenty minutes.

Text me if you need anything sooner."

Mac thanked her mom and slung her backpack over her shoulder. Tally followed her back to the Wheeler Ring. The first junior hunter class of the day had begun and Tally slowed down to gawp at the horse in the ring. It was a dark bay, all shiny mahogany and black, except for a perfect white star on its forehead. Approaching a two-stride set near the fence line, the rider audibly clucked at her horse and he snapped his knees up tight over the first jump, stretching through the two strides to the oxer. The jumps were absolutely massive.

"Can you imagine what it feels like to jump that big?" Tally asked her friend, who'd also slowed down to watch the action in the ring.

"I really can't! Looks like fun though."

Back in "pony land," as Mac called the Wheeler

Ring and surrounding areas, Tally and Mac watched the small pony hunters jump around the handy course. It was the same one Mac would be jumping, just set three inches lower at the moment. Spectators sat in bleachers and perched on the little grassy hill to the left of the Wheeler Ring. Tally couldn't contain her huge grin when the announcer named the pony and rider heading into the ring. She recognized the announcer's voice from all the horse show videos she'd been watching. Every word was enunciated just so, his voice like honey.

Sleepy-looking ponies stood near the in-gate with their grooms and riders. In the ring, one of the ponies was making a tight inside turn where there was also the option to go wider.

"That's the turn Ryan wants me to make," Mac said, her eyes glued on the ring. "I think it'll be fun."

A hint of a smile played at her mouth. The course also featured a trot jump and the girls watched as several ponies executed it well. One came very close to cantering a stride, but his little rider was dead-set on holding her trot and the pony jumped the fence well. The course also featured a brush jump at the end of the ring, one of the last jumps. It was a very long approach that tricked some riders into getting ahead of or behind the pace.

"You could have coffee by the time you get to that one," one spectator said to another with a laugh and a nod toward the brush. The pony and rider currently on course were having a tough time, adding a stride down one line and getting a late lead change before exiting the ring. They both looked relieved to be done.

"Score of fifty-five here, fifty-five," the announcer

declared. Tally thought it was good sportsmanship that the rider gave the pony a big pat despite her obvious frustration with the trip.

"That was a get-around ride. Survival," the spectator told the lady next to her. "Sometimes you just have to get around and the prize is something other than a ribbon."

Tally glanced at Mac, who'd obviously heard the commentary too. Maybe that was a good description of the day before for her and Joey. And hopefully today would be different.

As the small ponies' second class wrapped up and the results were announced, Mac put on her show coat and tied on her number. She checked her hairnet for any stray hairs and turned the collar of her show shirt up, snapping buttons around her neck.

Ryan walked over to the girls. "As soon as they

start the championship ceremony for the smalls, we'll get on," he said, and Mac nodded.

Tally felt more nervous than if she were showing herself while she watched Mac flat Joey around and then jump the plain white fences in the center of the schooling area.

Once Ryan gave Mac a firm, slow nod—often his signal that they were done schooling, Tally had noticed—they walked out of the ring and Mac dismounted, taking a sip from the water bottle her mom handed her.

"Watch a few go and then you'll hop back on," Ryan said. Mac's mom gave her a quick hug and wished her luck. Mac then turned to Tally with a tight-lipped smile. Tally winked at her friend before she spoke.

"You've got this, Tom Brady."

Mac let out an easy laugh and Tally was glad to help her friend relax, even if just for a moment. Tally couldn't imagine what this kind of show pressure felt like.

"You want me to go sit with your mom in the bleachers?"

"Sure," Mac said, eyes trained on the ring. "Thanks, Tal, I'm so glad you're here."

"Me too," Tally replied, giving her friend a quick hug. "Good luck!"

17

"Next to go in our handy hunter round for the medium ponies is number 285. This is Smoke Hill Jet Set, ridden by Mackenzie Bennett."

The sun hit Joey's chestnut coat as Mac walked him into the ring. He was positively gleaming. Mac took a visibly deep breath before picking up the canter just steps inside of the gate. Tally thought that was the coolest part of handy classes, how the ponies just got right to work, no time wasted with a circle or a tour around the ring.

"Ring pace," Tally whispered to herself as she watched Mac build Joey's canter to just where she needed it. Then it was only a few strides to the first jump, a birch single with a gate and pretty purple flowers in the boxes below. Joey jumped it adorably—they were off to a good start.

Tally, seriously nervous for her friend, had to remind herself to breathe, but Mac had her usual look of cool confidence as she piloted Joey around the beautiful, classic-looking jumps. As they approached the two-stride, Tally clucked under her breath, but Mac had exactly the step she needed today and they jumped in perfectly, Joey striking two easy strides in between the fences and jumping out clean. They had a single after that, and then the slick inside turn they'd watched a rider do in the small pony handy class. Just one stride after the single,

Mac sat up tall and shaped their inside turn, Joey's ears trained hard on the jump ahead. He gave it a round effort with plenty of clearance, and Mac kept his nice, open canter to the next jump, the second of a bending line.

All they had left was the trot jump, the long canter to the brush, and then the final oxer. Joey completed the trot jump with ease, as if he did them in his sleep. Mac got up out of the tack a little bit to build his canter back up and Joey responded eagerly, springing right back up to ring pace. Kids who were watching from the hill near the fence line looked to be getting restless—one was waving her arms around, clearly not a horse person herself, as no rider would do something to potentially spook the pony in the ring. Thankfully, Joey was focused in on the brush and didn't notice the crowd. They met the brush out of stride and sailed over the top. Mac made a right turn toward home for the last jump and her mom grabbed Tally's hand and squeezed it. Cindy wasn't a horse person either, but she'd learned a lot watching her daughter showing over the years. She knew this was a great round so far. Tally glanced over at her and then back at the ring, just in time to count the final three, two, one strides and then Joey easily cleared the fence. He landed on the correct lead and cantered away proudly, Mac immediately breaking into a huge smile. She pulled him up before the in-gate, walking the last couple of strides out.

At the gate, Ryan whistled and hollered for his pony and rider while Cindy and Tally shamelessly jumped to their feet, whooping and applauding. A couple of people turned to give them funny looks, but Tally couldn't have cared less. Mac laid down a trip worthy of a loud celebration.

"And that'll be a new high score here, folks, an eighty-six for Smoke Hill Jet Set, with Mackenzie Bennett in the irons."

Tally hurried over to congratulate her friend, catching the end of her talk with Ryan.

"Good riding, girl, way to stick with it! You rode so much smarter today and it's gonna pay off in the long run. Was it fun?"

Mac nodded happily and hugged Joey around the neck. They posed for photos in front of a huge wall of flowers adorned with the Devon logo. After several more trips, Mac and Joey's 86 was still the high score with eight more ponies to go. Could Mac win a class at Devon?

"Someone will beat an 86," Mac told Tally, as

if reading her mind. She did this fairly often. "But I'm just so happy. We fixed yesterday's disaster and Joey was perfect."

She gave the pony another hug before hopping off. Her mom was waiting with her shad belly, a special show coat with long tails that riders wore in stakes classes, which was next for the mediums.

After all the ponies had completed the handy course, Joey and Mac were called back to jog second—only one pony and rider had edged them out with a score of 87. Tally thought Mac and Joey's rosette was the most beautiful horse show ribbon she'd ever seen.

With the pressure off, Mac walked into the ring for her stakes class smiling. They had one tight distance jumping into a line, and Joey had to speed up and stretch a bit to get out in the correct number of strides. Other than that, they looked great to Tally.

"The score for Smoke Hill Jet Set and Mackenzie Bennett: seventy-five. Seven-five."

Tally saw Mac give a little shrug and Ryan nodded at her encouragingly. Mac's mom asked Tally why the score was lower than in the handy and Tally talked her through it.

"You really know your stuff, Tal. And Mac is lucky to have a friend like you. Thanks so much for coming."

Tally rejoined her friend, and they watched a few more trips and checked the live scoring on Tally's phone. As the class neared a close, it became clear that Joey would be just out of the ribbons, finishing twelfth out of the field of thirty. Mac's mom took her daughter's shad belly and Mac tucked her helmet inside her backpack.

"Let's go get some food," she said to Tally, smiling. The twelfth-place finish didn't seem to bother her in the least.

"Do you want me to take your ribbon, too?" Mac's mom asked.

"Heck no," her daughter replied and all three laughed. Hooking the red rosette with its fancy medallion on her jodhpur pocket, the girls set off to check out the fair. Mac's mom would be back in a couple of hours to pick them up. Passing the Dixon Oval, they took in a few more junior hunter rounds and then found the candy booth in the fair.

"Thanks for coming," Mac said, handing Tally a lemon with the top cut off, a yellow candy stick poking out the top.

"You're thanking me by making me drink a lemon?" Tally joked and tapped her fruit against Mac's. "Cheers?"

Mac laughed. "It's so good, I promise. Just try it," she said, demonstrating how to sip the lemon juice through the candy stick. And she was right. The sour of the lemon juice mixed with the sweetness of the candy stick made it a delicious and refreshing treat. Mac and Tally sipped their lemon sticks as they walked around the fair, also stopping to buy Devon's traditional tea sandwiches. They played a couple of fair games and rode the ferris wheel, looking down on the horse show from high above.

Back on the ground, Mac wanted to stop by the exhibitors' lounge to say goodbye to Ryan. She held the door open for Tally and got her an iced tea from a dispenser in the center of the room. Tally noticed baskets of giant carrot chunks and grabbed a few for Joey. Mac gave Ryan a hug and thanked him, and he waved to both girls as they headed to Joey's barn to say goodbye to him, too.

Both Mac and Tally had stuffed their pockets full of the fat carrots and they took turns feeding Joey, who happily turned from girl to girl to eat up the treats until it was time for them to head home.

"I love you," Mac whispered, kissing the side of Joey's face. "Thank you."

Keep Reading the *Show Strides* Series

Up Next:

#3 Moving Up and Moving On

About the Authors

Piper Klemm, Ph.D. is the publisher of *The Plaid Horse* magazine and a partner in The Plaid Horse Network. Additionally, she co-hosts the weekly podcast of The Plaid Horse, the #Plaidcast, and is an adjunct professor at St. Lawrence University. She has been riding since she was eight years old and currently owns a dozen hunter ponies who compete on the horse show circuit. She frequently competes in the adult hunter divisions across North America, so you might see her at a horse show near you!

Rennie Dyball has loved horses ever since she was a little girl. She started taking lessons at age twelve, went on to compete with the Penn State equestrian team, and continues to show in the hunter, jumper, and equitation rings. She spent fifteen years as a writer and editor at *People* magazine and People.com, and has ghostwritten several books. With *Show Strides*, Rennie is thrilled to combine two of her greatest passions—writing and riding.

About the Illustrator

Madeleine Murray grew up in rural Vermont, among horses and working farms. She is a painter and illustrator based in northern New York, as well as an artist-in-residence at *The Plaid Horse* magazine. You can see her paintings at mmurrayart.com.

Who's Who at Quince Oaks

Ava Foster: Friends with Tally and Kaitlyn, used to own Danny but quits riding.

Beau: Field Ridge pony who belongs to a rider named Marion

Brenna: Barn manager at Quince Oaks

Cindy Bennett: Mac's mom

Field Ridge: Ryan's business within Quince Oaks

Goose: A green small pony that Tally is catch-riding

Isabelle: Sixteen-year-old who rides with Ryan

James Hart: Tally's dad

Jordan: Takes lessons at Quince Oaks, sometimes with Tally

Kaitlyn Rowe: Tally's best friend at school

Kelsey: Working student for the riding school

Mackenzie (Mac) Bennett: Newcomer to the barn who owns Joey

Maggie: Takes lessons at Quince Oaks, sometimes with Tally

Marsha: the barn secretary at Quince Oaks

Meg: Tally's instructor at Quince Oaks before Ryan

Quince Oaks: The barn

Ryan McNeil: Mackenzie's trainer and Tally's new instructor after Meg leaves the barn.

Scout: One of the Quince Oaks school horses

Smoke Hill Jet Set (Joey at the barn): Mac's medium pony hunter

Stacy Hart: Tally's mom

Stonelea Dance Party (Danny at the barn): Formerly Ava Foster's pony, goes up for sale through Ryan

Sweet Talker (Sweetie at the barn): Tally's favorite school horse

Natalia (Tally) Hart: Rides Ryan's sales ponies and in the lesson program at Quince Oaks

Glossary of Horse Terminology

A circuit: Nationally-rated horse shows.

backed: When a horse or pony that's newly in training has a rider on its back for the first time.

base: Where a horse or pony leaves the ground in front of a jump; also: refers the rider's feet in the stirrups, with heels down acting as anchors, or a base of support, for the rider's legs.

bay: A horse color that consists of a brown coat and black points (i.e., black mane, tail, ear edges and legs).

canter: A three-beat gait that horses and ponies travel in-it's a more controlled version of the gallop, the fastest of the gaits (which are walk, trot, canter, gallop.)

cavaletti: Very small jumps for schooling, or jumping practice.

chestnut: A reddish brown horse/pony coat color, with a lighter mane and tail.

chip: When a horse or pony takes off too close to a jump by adding in an extra stride near the base.

colt: A young male horse.

conformation class: A horse show class in which the animals are modeled and judged on their build.

crest release: When the rider places his or her hands up the horse or pony's neck, thus adding slack to the reins and giving the animal freedom of movement in its head and neck.

crop/bat: A small (and humane!) whip that is used behind the rider's leg when the rider's leg aid is not sufficient.

cross-rail: A jump consisting of two rails in the shape of an X.

curry comb: A grooming tool used in circles on a horse or pony's coat to lift out dirt.

Devon: An annual, prestigious invitation-only horse show in Pennsylvania.

diagonal line: Two jumps with a set distance between them set on the diagonal of a riding ring.

distance: The take-off spot for a jump. Riders often talk about "finding distances," which means finding the ideal spot to take off over a jump.

flower boxes: Like "walls," these are jump adornments that are placed below the lowest rail of a jump.

gate: Part of a jump that is placed in the jump cups instead of a rail. Typically heavier than a standard jump rail so horses and ponies can be more careful in jumping them to as not to hit a hoof.

gelding: A castrated male horse.

girth: A piece of equipment that holds the saddle securely on a horse or pony. The girth attaches to the billets under the flaps of the saddle and goes underneath the horse, behind the front legs, and is secured on the billets on the other side.

green: A horse or pony who has less training and/or experience (the opposite of a "made" horse or pony, which has lots of training and experience).

gymnastic: A line of jumps with one, two, or zero strides between them (no strides in between jumps is called a bounce — the horse or pony lands, and the horse or pony lands off the first jump and immediately takes off for the next without taking a stride).

hack: Can either mean riding a horse on the flat (no jumps) in an indoor ring or outside; or, an under-saddle class at a horse show, in which the animal is judged on its performance on the flat.

hands: A unit of measurement for horse or pony heights. One hand equals 4 inches so a 15-hand horse is 60 inches tall from the ground to its withers. A pony that's 12.2 hands is 12 hands, 2 inches, or 50 inches tall at the withers.

handy: A handy class in a hunter division is meant to test a horse or pony's handiness, or its ability to navigate a course. Special elements included in handy hunter courses may include trot jumps, roll backs and hand gallops.

in-gate: Sometimes just referred to as "the gate," it's where horses enter and exit the show ring. Usually it's one gate for both directions; sometimes two gates will be in use, one to go in and the other to come out.

large pony: A pony that measures over 13.2 hands but no taller than 14.2 hands.

lead changes: Changing of the canter lead from right to left or vice versa. The inside front and hind legs stretch farther when the horse or pony is on the correct lead. A lead change can be executed in two ways: A simple lead change is when the horse transitions from the canter to the trot and then picks up the opposite canter lead. In a flying lead change, the horse changes its lead in midair without trotting.

line: Two jumps with a set number of strides between them.

longe line: A long lead that attaches to a horse's halter or bridle. The horse or pony travels around the handler in a large circle to work on the flat with commands from the handler holding the line.

Maclay: One of the big equitation or "big eq" classes for junior riders. Riders compete in regional Maclay classes to qualify for the annual Maclay Final. The final is currently held at the National Horse Show at the Kentucky Horse Park in the fall.

mare: A mature female horse.

martingale: A piece of tack intended to keep a horse or pony from raising its head too high. The martingale attaches to the girth, between the animal's front legs, and then (in a standing martingale) a single strap attaches to the noseband or (in a running martingale) a pair of straps attach to the reins.

medium pony: A pony taller than 12.2 hands but no taller than 13.2 hands.

outside line: A line of jumps with a set number of strides between them on the long sides of the riding ring. An outside line set parallel to the judges' box/stand is called a judges' line.

oxer: A type of jump that features two sets of standards and two top rails, which can be set even (called a square oxer) or uneven, with the back rail higher than the front. A typical hunter over fences class features single oxers as well as oxers set as the "out" jump in lines.

palomino: A horse or pony with a golden color coat and a white mane and tail.

pinned: The way a horse show class is ordered and ribbons are awarded, typically from first through sixth or first through eight place (though some classes go to tenth or even twentieth place).

polos: Also called polo wraps, they provide protection and support to a horse or pony's legs while being ridden.

pommel: The front part of an English saddle; the rider sits behind this.

posting trot: When a rider posts (stands up and sits down in the saddle) as the horse or pony is trotting, making the gait more comfortable and less bouncy for both the rider and the animal.

quarter sheet: A blanket intended for cold weather riding that attaches under the saddle flaps and loops under the horse or pony's tail.

regular pony hunter division (sometimes called "the division"): A national, or A-rated horse show division in which small ponies jump 2'3, medium ponies jump 2'6, and large ponies jump 2'9-3'.

rein: The reins are part of the bridle and attach to the horse or pony's bit. Used for steering and slowing down.

sales pony/sales horse: A pony or horse that is offered for sale; trainers often market a sales horse or pony through ads and by showing the animal.

school horses/school ponies: Horses or ponies who are used in a program teaching riding lessons.

schooling ring: A ring at a horse show designated for warming up or schooling.

schooling shows: Unrated shows intended for practice as well as for green horses and ponies to gain experience.

shad belly: A formal show coat with tails typically worn for hunter classics and derbies.

small pony: A pony that measures 12.2 hands and under.

spooky: A horse or pony that's acting easily spooked or startled.

spurs: An artificial aid, worn on a rider's boots to add impulsion.

stakes class: Part of a hunter division; it's a class that offers prize money.

stirrup irons: The metal loops in which riders place their feet.

stirrup leathers: Threaded through the stirrup bars of the saddle and through the stirrups themselves, the leathers hold the stirrups in place.**swap**: When a horse or pony unnecessarily changes its lead on course.

tack: The equipment a horse wears to be ridden (e.g. saddle, bridle, martingale, etc.).

trail rides: A ride that takes places out on trails instead of in a riding ring.

transition: When a horse or pony moves from one gait to another, for example, moving from the canter to the trot is a downward transition; moving from the walk to the trot is an upward transition.

trot: A two-beat gait in which the horse or pony's legs move in diagonal pairs.

tricolors: The ribbons awarded for champion (most points in a division) and reserve champion (second highest number of points in that division).

trip: Another term for a jumping round, or course, mostly used at shows, as in, "the pony's first trip."

vertical: A jump that includes one set of standards and a rail or rails set horizontally.

The Plaid Horse encourages every young equestrian to:

- **Read** *The Plaid Horse* magazine and online at theplaidhorse.com/read

  Subscribe at theplaidhorse.com/subscribe

- **Watch** The Plaid Horse Network at network.theplaidhorse.com

  On Roku, AppleTV, The Plaid Horse Network App for iOS & Android

- **Listen** to the #Plaidcast, The Podcast of The Plaid Horse at   theplaidhorse.com/listen

  On iTunes, Google Play, Stitcher, & Spotify